# Codename Icarus

*"Smith: you are a dirty, m..., clown."*

*Martin Smith's parents had been to see his Head-master. Again. The same grumbles, the same complaints, the same feeling of the sour defeat of all their hopes for the boy.*

*"Word is that you're thick. You know that, don't you?"*
*"Should do sir. I've been told often enough."*

How then does Martin Smith gain a place at Falconleigh, a school for children gifted in science and maths, and part of the mysterious Icarus Foundation? And who is the enigmatic figure behind Icarus, and what are his aims?

# CODENAME
# ICARUS

Richard Cooper

BBC/KNIGHT

Copyright © Richard Cooper 1981
First published 1981 by the
British Broadcasting Corporation and
Knight Books


**British Library C.I.P.**

Cooper, Richard
    Codename Icarus.—(Knight books)
    I. Title
    823´.914[F]        PR6053.057/

    ISBN 0 340 27535 9
    ISBN 0 563 20040 5 (BBC)

---

Filmset by Rowland Phototypesetting Ltd.,
Bury St Edmunds, Suffolk. Printed
and bound in Great Britain for
the British Broadcasting Corporation,
35 Marylebone High Street, London W1M 4AA
and Hodder and Stoughton Paperbacks, a
division of Hodder and Stoughton Ltd.,
Mill Road, Dunton Green, Sevenoaks,
Kent (Editorial Office: 47 Bedford
Square, London, WC1 3DP) by
Cox & Wyman, Reading.

*For the begetters . . .*
*Anna, Paul, Marilyn and Sheila*

*And, one day, for Jenny, Sarah Jane and Jack*

# ONE

Mr Evans threw his blackboard duster on to the table and a cloud of chalk dust rose and fell in a beam of bright sunlight: Martin picked out one speck and followed the pattern it made in the air. It was something to pass the time, and anything was better than listening to the boringness of the teacher as he heaved IVb through the swamp of quadratic equations. The classroom was still, the children holding heavy heads on their cupped hands, faces pulled and twisted. It was the first lesson after dinner; the next would be more lively, and the teacher would really have to work at it when they came to the last period of the afternoon. It was a day, in fact, as empty of interest as any other that fell to Martin in that school.

Martin's particle of chalk settled on his desk; he leant forward, looking at it so closely that he quite forgot about the rest of the classroom—it was as if it had all disappeared —scratched desks, worn books, figure-covered blackboard. That dot of chalk held more interest for him than any or all of it. Then, suddenly, a hand slammed down in front of him, and all the patterns were broken. He looked up, angry, and saw that the girl whose wide back was usually his shield against the teacher's prying eyes, had turned round in her seat and was grinning at him.

"What's the big joke, then?" he whispered.

"Well might you ask, Smith," Evans cried, high above the giggling and shuffling of the rest of the class, "well might you ask!"

Martin considered the sound of the teacher's voice—he didn't sound *too* angry, a quick word of apology might head him off. "Sorry, sir," he said, almost sounding as if he meant it.

"Oh, don't be sorry," Evans grinned, definitely *not* meaning it. "I'm sure you've been paying close attention all the time . . ."

"Sir," Martin nodded.

"And you can show us, can't you Smith, just how carefully you've been following this lesson?"

"Yes, sir."

There was a ripple of expectant laughter from the kids: Martin Smith was their clown, and here he was, ambling to the centre of the ring.

"Shut up, you lot!" Evans shouted. And then: "Come here, Smith."

Martin walked along the line of desks and stood in front of him, hands behind his back, head down and a length of uncombed hair hanging over his eyes.

"Know what that is?" Evans asked, pointing to the blackboard.

"Yes, sir. It's an equation, sir."

"Clever lad! That's *very* good! An *equation*!" He mouthed the word slowly, as if it had been something rich and original. "Well, that's very nearly right, isn't it? An *equation*. For it *will* be just that . . . *when you've completed it*! Here you are, Smith, here's the chalk . . ."

Martin took the piece of chalk and stood, turning it over and over in his hand, looking at the lines of figures and letters, each one drooping downwards at the end, as if they were giving up hope.

"We're waiting . . ."

Martin glanced at the other kids and grinned, asking for support.

"Funny, is it?" Evans shouted, his face near Martin's. His breath smelled of peppermint.

The class laughed, sitting up now, excited by Martin's danger.

Evans turned on them. "You think it's funny too, do you? Well, get what laughs you can out of this . . . if this idiot doesn't get this equation right, you'll all be here half an hour after school. Is that funny?"

They were quiet now, staring at Martin and not liking him. Evans walked to the back of the room, enjoying the situation. That kid could sweat it out: he deserved to.

He stood at the back of the class, reading, as if with great interest, the notices on the pin board. Behind him he could hear the raw squeak of chalk. He turned round very slowly; the boy was standing in front of an untidy scrawl of figures.

"What's that supposed to be, Smith?" he shouted, leaning against the wall.

"The answer, sir," Martin muttered, his head still bowed.

"The *what*? What did you say it was, lad?"

"The answer!"

Evans let a moment of silence go by. "I see. Well now . . ." He walked to the front, coming in fast for the kill, picking up the teacher's text book, already open at the answer page, from his desk. His eyes flicked to the book, to the blackboard, and then to Martin. He threw the book back on to his desk and moved closer to the lad, bending so that his face was only inches away. "You cheated, didn't you, Smith?" He grabbed Martin's hair, pulling his head up and back. "Looked at my book?" His voice was low, angry, the Welsh accent beating through.

9

"No, sir."

"Liar!"

"I didn't cheat! Never even saw your rotten book!"

"Sir!" Evans roared.

Martin took a deep breath. "Sir . . ."

Evans let go of him and sat on the edge of his desk, searching for words that would hurt.

"Listen, lout. I studied the science of mathematics for four years at my university. At the end of that time they thought that I was all right; gave me a good degree. So: I am a *mathematician*, Smith—not that you'd have the faintest idea what that means. But I'll tell you this; to complete that equation without going through all the stages would be very difficult, even for me . . . but for a clown like you . . ."

*"I didn't cheat!"*

Evans shoved him to one side, walked to the blackboard, picked up the duster and, as if he were rubbing a dirty slogan off a wall, wiped Martin's figures away. Then he faced him again. "Smith: you are a dirty, messy, stupid, lying clown." He turned to the rest of the class. "Isn't he?"

They grinned back. One or two of them nodded.

"See?" he said, very quietly, to Martin. Then he took the duster and slowly pressed it against the boy's face, making his cheeks white. "So . . . now you got your make-up. Happy?"

The class laughed, but Martin didn't speak, looking at Evans expressionlessly. Then he turned away, walked back to his place and sat down, not looking at his neighbours or making any move to wipe the white patches from his face. Other lessons happened, and teachers looked at him enquiringly, but he offered no explanation.

Now detention time was over: the master stood and dismissed the class. There was an angry slamming of books into canvas bags, brief-cases, satchels, and the deafening screech of thirty chairs being pushed back. "Quietly, now!" he shouted and stood by the door to watch them out.

As the kids walked down the corridor, two of the biggest lads pushed themselves to either side of Martin and then shouldered him, one to the other and back again. No one objected—it was all Martin's fault—everyone knew that.

Martin stopped, turned, and started elbowing his way back through the crowd.

"Where do you think *you're* going, Smithy?" one of the lads shouted.

"Forgotten my homework book," he replied.

A girl near to him laughed in his face, and her friend tried to trip him up.

"Chicken!" several of them shouted.

"That's enough of that!" the master bellowed from the classroom door. Then he grabbed Martin's arm. "What's the matter with you, Smith? Don't you want to go home?"

"I've lost one of my books, sir . . . it's in there somewhere . . ."

"Can't you get it tomorrow?"

"Need it tonight, sir, for my homework."

"All right: hurry up. And don't leave that room in a mess, Smith, or I'll have your guts for garters first thing in the morning . . ." And the master walked quickly to catch up with the rest of IVB, anxious to see them off the premises, and to get home to his tea. Smith would be safe enough in the classroom—best place for him in fact, for the next ten minutes. There wasn't any damage he could do that hadn't already been done, and, God knows, there was nothing there worth pinching.

Until the sounds of the voices died away, Martin banged the books in his desk about a bit. Then the school was quiet, except for the singing of a cleaning lady working a floor polisher, but she was a long way off.

He walked to the door and quietly closed it, then turned to look at the blackboard. Evans had partly cleaned it, but ghosts of weary sums glimmered through a mist of chalk. Martin went to the board and cleaned it properly and carefully, with long, straight sweeps of the duster.

That made him feel a lot better.

He stood, eyes closed, all of his concentration in his listening. It was safe: the cleaner was further off, and there was no other sound.

Taking care to make no noise, he pulled the teacher's desk a couple of feet nearer the door, then, just as quietly, he put a chair on top of it. After a moment of listening to make sure that no one was coming, he climbed on to the desk, on to the chair and stretched his arms up, pushing against one of the large polystyrene ceiling tiles. It swung up and away from him, and a gust of cold dusty air blew down on him from the roof void. By standing on tiptoe he was able to get his hands on to the joists and then, with a giant heave, he pulled himself up and into the roof.

He sat on the edge of the hole that was now in the ceiling, pulled a long length of string from his pocket and made sure that the piece of wire that he'd bent into a hook was still securely fastened to the end of it. He let the string slip slowly through his fingers, swinging the hook to catch the back of the chair. After a couple of attempts he managed it and gently pulled until the chair was lifted from the table. Now came the difficult bit, as he swung the chair away from the table and down to the ground. Then he unhooked his string and pulled it back up, wrapping it round and round his hand and putting it back into his pocket. He replaced the ceiling tile.

Once again it had worked—he was safe.

He looked along the huge space of the roof; the whole length of one wing of the school lay before him, with the triangles of the roof supports going off into the distance, getting smaller and smaller.

Slowly, on all fours, taking care to put his weight only on the joists, he crawled along the space, whispering the names of the classrooms over which he was passing.

"Geography . . . Chemistry . . . Physics . . . Biology."

He stopped and, more cautiously than ever, lowered himself down to peer through a small hole in a tile beneath him. Satisfied, he lifted the tile, placed it to one side, lowered his legs through the space and, grasping the joists, dropped down to a workbench. Silently he slipped to the ground, walked over to the door and made sure that it was locked.

The room was his now, for as long as he wanted it; and, in the very centre of it was the object of his dangerous journey; pride of the school, forbidden to everyone except the science and maths specialists of the sixth form, white, gleaming, powerful.

The computer.

His feelings, as he stood before it, were like those of the priest at the altar. With this thing he was whole and complete—without it, he was a sly and stupid clown.

He held the moment, enjoying it, then walked over to the machine, flicked the "on" switch and rested his hands on the keyboard, letting them absorb the vibrating impulses. For the first time that day, he was happy.

He took a roll of papers from his inside pocket, spread them on the bench at the side of the screen and studied them, frowning slightly. Then, quickly and expertly, he began to tap out a long and complex mathematical formula. The figures and symbols flashed on to the screen—ordered, patterned and beautiful.

*

Martin's parents were at a loss, not knowing which way to turn. It was terrible for them to want to help him so much and to be so unable to do it. They couldn't admit that they didn't know him, but talking to him was like talking to a stranger, and when other people spoke to them about their son it was like a stranger being discussed. That afternoon they had been to see his Headmaster. Again. The same grumbles, the same complaints, the same feeling of the sour defeat of all their hopes for the boy. If it weren't for the fact that their other son, Martin's older brother, Barry, was the shining star of the same school, they'd have felt that somehow it was all their fault that Martin was drifting further and further down and no one was able to stop him.

They hadn't said much on the journey home, nor while Mrs Smith was making tea, or now while they ate it. As had so often happened lately, there were just the three of them round the table, with Martin's empty place between them.

Mr Smith sipped at his second cup of tea and looked across at his wife. "God knows where he gets to every night—I'm sure I don't," he said.

"Bird-watching. That's what he says," she replied. "It *is* his hobby . . . and he takes those binoculars of his with him every day, that I *do* know . . ."

"Bird-watching!" Barry laughed. "Two-legged sort if you ask me!"

"What do you mean?" Mr Smith asked.

"He means lasses, and he's wrong. He'd have been nattering for some more pocket money if it'd been owt to do with lasses. He hasn't been, so it's not."

Barry shrugged his shoulders. "Suit yourselves then." He got up from the table. "Want me to keep an eye on him? I'd soon find out."

Mr Smith shook his head. "I'll not have anyone spying

on one of my children. Not even you, Barry."

"OK. Then you'd best buy him a budgie. He can sit at home and watch that." And he went towards the door.

"Where you off to, then?" his mother asked.

"Training. See you later."

"Kids!" Mr Smith said, as the door slammed.

"Aye," his wife replied.

*

Martin was once more in the computer room: this time, he promised himself, he would keep a careful eye on the time—last night he'd had to dodge pretty fast to avoid the school caretaker—then, when he got home, he'd run into the usual cross-fire of questioning. So he took his wrist watch off (present from Auntie Elsie if he moved up in class at the Christmas exams, and he had, from thirtieth to twenty-ninth, out of thirty), and carefully placed it beside him.

Half an hour—that's what he'd give himself—then home.

He took the papers from his pocket, but he was afraid to put them to the test. When he'd been in bed, and during all the lessons at school, he'd been thinking of this new idea: numbers and symbols being hammered together into shapes and combinations that no one had ever even dreamed of before.

But . . . supposing that they didn't work out? Supposing that he couldn't make them stick, and it had all been a waste of time; stupid, idle dreaming?

He took a deep breath and switched the machine on. There was only one way to find out. The light of the screen shone into his eyes. His hands were sweating and he wiped them on a crumpled ball of paper tissue. This was the very worst moment: he was the high-wire walker on the platform, waiting to take the first step over empty space.

He rested his hands on the keyboard and forced himself to tap out the first line. Then it was done, the figures were before him. He was committed.

He carefully checked the calculation. So far, all right. It had to lead to the next line . . . it *had* to! The formula was a road that dipped out of sight over a hill, but it must be there again, on the other side of the valley, ready to be walked.

The calculations went on, and he was almost unaware that he was writing them. He worked faster and faster until, at last, he came to the finishing line. As if he were angry, he pushed his chair away and walked to the other side of the room, not looking at the screen.

He felt a little bit sick and he would have liked to have opened a window; but he didn't dare. Very slowly, he turned to face his work and deliberately slowed his mind to a walk through the steps that he had taken, mentally ticking them off, and he had a memory of a wonderful teacher he'd had in infant school, and the neat red ticks that she'd flicked at the side of his sums. It was all right—every stage was good.

It worked! IT WORKED!

Then he remembered the time. He ran over to his watch and groaned aloud when he saw that he'd been there for more than an hour. He shuffled his papers together, found a blank space on one of them and started to write, glancing occasionally at the screen to verify a figure. It was while his head was down and he was writing that, out of the corner of his eye, he thought that he saw a change in the pattern on the screen. Startled, he looked up and saw that it was indeed different now. Beneath his last line was one word . . . and he hadn't put it there. It simply said BEAUTIFUL.

He held his breath, frightened at what this meant. Someone had made a connection with *his* computer, someone had been watching all the time, following his mind, *in* his mind.

But who?

It couldn't be anyone in the school—this was the only computer they had, so he was safe there.

Where then?

Another line appeared on the screen: PLEASE IDENTIFY.

He lurched away, to the side of the machine, as if whoever was there could see him through the screen.

It came again: REPEAT PLEASE IDENTIFY.

That was it: no more hesitation or need for thought. He dived for the plug, pulled it from the socket, bundled his papers up and escaped as fast as he could, back into the roof.

The machine was silent in the empty room.

\*

Martin's father was waiting in the kitchen, sitting on one of the plastic-topped stools, drinking a cup of coffee. It was his third cup, but that didn't bother him. He was a very patient man. He heard the front door open, then the creak of the floorboard by the hallstand. He put down his cup and walked to the kitchen door.

"Hello, Martin," he said.

Martin stopped, one foot on the bottom stair. Mr Smith looked up at his son's white face—as if he's seen a ghost, he thought.

"I'm sorry I'm late, Dad."

"We were worried—mind you, we're getting a bit used to worrying."

Martin didn't say anything to that, but started to walk upstairs.

"Well?"

He turned to look down at his father.

17

"What?"

"Nothing . . ." Mr Smith said, and walked back into the kitchen.

*

It wasn't just Evans who didn't think much of Martin, none of the teachers did.

Even Anderson could find little to say in his favour, and anyone who couldn't get on with *him*, couldn't get on with any teacher. As his class worked, he looked across at the lad. He noted the shock of hair falling into his eyes, the knot of his tie somewhere under his collar, the dusty blazer. If you didn't know the family, Anderson thought, you'd think that the kid lived on the town rubbish dump. How on earth did he get like that?

Just now, while everyone else was writing, Smith sat, staring at a pencil that he was moving, very slowly, from one side of his desk to the other. Anderson pushed himself up from his chair and walked along the file of desks towards him. Still the lad didn't notice him, but kept moving the pencil, as if it were the only important thing in the world. Not for the first time, Anderson wondered if Martin Smith shouldn't be referred to the school psychologist.

He picked up Martin's exercise book and now, at last, the lad was aware of him, looking up, but unsurprised, unstartled, his eyes, as always, having that strange quality, seeming to look inwards rather than out. Anderson glanced at the blank page—nothing done. Twenty minutes of lesson time and not a mark to show for it!

He bent near to Martin. "What *do* you think you're playing at, Smith?" he whispered.

"Thinking, sir."

Anderson nodded. "What about, lad?"

Martin looked at the essay title on the blackboard. "That, sir."

"Don't just *think* about it, lad! Write something down. Anything! Just try . . . will you?"

Martin bent his head and started to write and Anderson walked back to his desk. No, he thought, I don't really know about Martin Smith.

That was the last lesson of the day and now it was finished. Exercise books were handed forwards, some kids giving the neighbour in front a slap on the head with the books as they were passed. Anderson piled them neatly on his desk, then took Martin's out. "Right," he said. "The rest of you can go. Smith, you stay here."

So Martin sat, while the rest of the class swung their bags on to their shoulders and crowded through the door.

Anderson came to Martin and sat on the desk in front of him, the exercise book in his hands. For a while he didn't say anything, but read over what Martin had written. Then he looked down at him, shaking his head slightly.

"Word is," he said, quietly and seriously, "that you're thick. You know that, don't you?"

"Should do, sir. I've been told often enough."

"Right. It's not true, though. Is it?"

Martin shrugged his shoulders, not meeting Anderson's gaze.

"This bit of writing you've done—and it *is* a bit, too—it's not bad. Spelling's all to pot, and the punctuation's non-existent, but just listen to what you've written here . . . 'the bird is not a creature who happens to be in the air like I happen to be in the water when I go swimming. It *is* the air itself and when it dies it should go back to the air, as I, being of the earth will become the earth . . .'"

"Birds are my hobby. Watching them."

"Are they now? Well . . . that's very good. Not that I asked you to write about birds, by the way, or your hobbies. But you've certainly showed that you're not thick. So you're not fooling me, not for a second."

Martin looked up at him quickly, then his head went down again.

"Your brother Barry, now: good lad, captain of the school, off to P.E. college when he's done his "A" Levels . . . but you know, and I know, that you could buy him and sell him . . . if you wanted to. Right?"

Martin didn't answer.

"This is what I want you to do, then—and it isn't a punishment, nothing like that. I want you to sit there and write me twelve more lines of this. That's all—just get to the bottom of the page. Will you do that?"

"If you like." There wasn't much enthusiasm in Martin's voice.

"I'll come back in half an hour; see how you're getting on." Anderson was already walking towards the door. "Don't forget now, no one's punishing you . . ."

Martin smiled, sourly, and looked at what he had written. He got no joy from it. Words to him were clumsy, clouded in many meanings, elusive as smoke. They could never say what he wanted to say, never hold the thrilled thought. Heavily, he wrote a couple of lines, but his mind began to drift away from the task and back to what had occupied him all day: the mystery of the computer room. Someone knew his mind, someone had broken into that secret fortress.

He wouldn't go in there again, not now. He would have to manage without the computer. The work would be painful and slow; weeks of calculations could be done in minutes with the machine, but there seemed to be no alternative. Then again, without the computer it wouldn't be long before someone would find out what he was spending so much time on—then everyone would know. He had a picture of Evans' clumsy hands rifling through his papers, of his lack of understanding of what he would read, of his smirching the beauty of his thought. That couldn't be faced. It couldn't.

Should he give the work up; try to be one with everyone else? But that was impossible—he had to go on.

So: he would have to take the risk and go back to the computer. And, after all, he told himself, maybe it wouldn't happen again, maybe what happened was some sort of accident or fluke. . . .

# TWO

Anderson came back into the classroom, but there was no sign of Martin, except for the exercise book, left open on the boy's desk. Anderson picked up the book and glanced over the work—it wasn't much further on than when he last saw it. At the foot of the page, Martin had written: "Sir, I can't stay any longer as I have a job to do for my father. Martin Smith IVB."

Does he really expect me to believe that, Anderson wondered? No—it had to be faced—there was no doing anything with Martin Smith. He was beyond help.

*

Now that Martin was in the computer room, he couldn't find the courage to switch on the machine. He stood, staring at it, anxiously biting at a thumb nail. Once, he decided to give up the whole thing and go home, and he got as far as climbing on the bench to get out.

But he knew that that was no answer, and he dropped back on to the floor, walked over to the plug, put it in and switched on. Better not hesitate now, he thought, and he started work straight away, punching out the first line of the problem. After that, it became easier: the theory to be tested was, after all, the important thing. He worked on, twice taking wrong turnings and having to retrace his steps, until, at last, he came to the end of it. Not that there could be any real conclusion, just an indication of the mountain of conjecture and work that waited to be climbed.

He was tired, and he had a headache behind his right eye. He leant back in the chair, trying to make a scheme for the next step in the work. That wasn't easy—could the answer lie in what he had just done? He went back over it carefully, tapping the lines on the screen with his pencil, looking for the hidden clue.

Then, suddenly, the eavesdropper was with him again —another line of figures appeared on the screen. It was a possible continuation of his work—though Martin knew that, if he followed it, it would lead to a dead end.

He wasn't as frightened now as he had been before. Whoever was watching him was a mathematician, not some nark of the Headmaster's. And that thought gave him a lot of comfort. Was there any point, even, in switching the set off? Whoever was out there wasn't doing any harm, and he still didn't know who Martin was. And it would be something to be able to talk to someone in his own language.

He touched the keys lightly, as if he were whispering, and tapped out a line which exposed the error in the other's thinking. Then he sat back, smiling slightly, waiting for this other mind to work through the reasoning and respond to the correction.

At last it came: a solitary "?"

Martin wrote again, trying to show a true way forward. This time a single set of his figures was picked out by the stranger, and after it appeared the single phrase DANGER-OUS PATH?

Martin laughed aloud and shook his head. NEGATIVE, he wrote.

Once more "?" came up on the screen.

Martin's problem now was one of communication—how to show, in small space and time, what might lie ahead. He punched out a symbol representing impossibility.

The stranger saw the point and put up a "!"

POSITIVE, Martin replied.

Then they came to the danger point once more.

PLEASE IDENTIFY, the stranger asked.

But this time Martin was ready for him.

EDWARD FROELICH, he wrote, knowing that whoever was out there would know that, brilliant as Froelich had been, he was dead: that great mathematician had been killed in an RAF raid on Germany in 1943.

? ? ? ? ? ? ? flashed across the screen, and Martin, enjoying the joke added one more "?" to the row.

CONTINUE TOMORROW? appeared.

POSITIVE, Martin replied, and switched the computer off.

*

Barry had a great sense of discipline and a love of routine. Every night he followed the same pattern; home by half-past four, a cup of coffee in the kitchen, then upstairs to his homework until teatime, half an hour's television after tea, then into his track suit for an hour's jogging. And, even when he jogged, he always took the same route—up to the park, across the piece (which was a bit of waste land used by the kids in the neighbourhood as a playground), and then back home again. It might rain, it might snow, the sun might even shine, but Barry kept to his time and his path.

It was as he was coming away from the piece that he saw Martin in the distance; head down, hurrying towards home. "Hey! Our kid!" he shouted.

Martin stopped and turned. "What?" he shouted back.

"I'll give you 'what'! Just stay there!"

So Martin stood where he was until Barry came up to him. "What's up?" he asked.

"Supposing you told me," Barry replied.

"Don't know what you mean."

"No?"

"Course not."

"Well, to start wi', what the thumping heck are you doing in the flamin' University library every night?"

"Who said I . . ."

"Never you mind! Come on! I asked you a question!"

Martin looked down at the ground, but Barry took his chin and pulled his head up until he was looking in his eyes.

"Let go! You're hurting!" Martin cried.

"When you've told us."

"It's to do wi' school . . . a project."

"What project would that be, like?"

"English . . . for Anderson."

"You daft little beggar! Who d'you think you're kidding! You don't do English projects in the Physics section!"

Martin tried to struggle away from him; but Barry had a very strong grip and held him easily. "It's my business," Martin cried, as he squirmed.

"I'm not saying it isn't—but what's all the flamin' secrecy for?"

"I've said . . ."

"I know what you've said! At least you can tell us what you're up to! That's not too much to ask, is it?"

It was some time before Martin answered him, and, when he did, he was so guarded, so shut in, that Barry didn't know if he was telling him the truth or not.

"It's some work . . . of my own."

"Oh aye?"

"Anyway, how did you find out?"

"I've some mates in the University athletics squad—one of them's seen you."

"Have you told Mam and Dad?"

"I'm leaving that for you, and I'll give you till I get home to do it." He shoved Martin away so hard that the boy would have gone sprawling if Barry hadn't grabbed an arm to steady him. "I sometimes wonder if you're all right in the head, I do. Physics! You!"

Now that Barry had let him go, Martin turned and ran, heavy haversack bumping and swinging as he went.

*

His Mam and Dad were watching television when they heard the sound of Martin's room door closing.

"Sounds as if he's back," his Mam said. Mr Smith got up and walked towards the door. "Tell him his tea's in the oven," she added.

Mr Smith hadn't meant to take Martin by surprise, catch him out, but he was wearing his slippers and he hadn't made a sound as he went up the stairs. Now, as he stood in the bedroom doorway, he was hurt by the look of angry contempt that Martin gave him. His son was standing on a chair, shoving something away on top of the wardrobe.

"Didn't mean to surprise you," Mr Smith said.

Martin made no reply, but stood quite still, staring at his father.

"Hiding something?" Mr Smith asked, but there was still no reply from Martin. "I'm sorry about that. I wouldn't have thought that you'd have needed to . . . in your own house. And you'd best get down off that chair, before you fall down."

Martin did as he was told and stood, facing him.

"It's . . ." he began to say, but couldn't finish.

"What . . . ?"

"Something . . . for me."

His father nodded. " 'Course it is—else why keep it from the rest of us?"

Martin was holding a book; tightly, arms folded across it.

"That book—I want to have a look at it, Martin. Please."

Martin backed away from him. "No Dad, no!" he whispered.

"Ashamed?"

"It's not that . . ."

"Well, then?"

"I've got to, haven't I, though . . .?" Mr Smith lifted an eyebrow, but otherwise didn't reply. "Then you'll tell everyone."

"Listen, Martin: as far as I'm concerned, no one's telling anyone anything—if you don't want them to."

"Promise?"

"Yes. I promise."

Martin shoved the book towards him. "Here you are then."

His father frowned as he turned the book over, reading the title on the spine: *Particle and anti-particle: a Critique of the Work of Gell–Mann.* He looked across at his son. "What do you want with this, Martin?"

In reply, Martin took the bundle of papers from his inside pocket and gave them to him.

Mr Smith knew the handwriting immediately. "Yours?" he asked.

Martin nodded.

His father looked at the papers, at the page after page of formulae and calculations. "You copying this stuff out, or what? Out of this book?"

"No. I'm not. I'm shoving the work in that book on a bit. He's out of date."

His father was completely lost now. *"You're what?"* he gasped.

Martin felt sorry for him, knowing that he couldn't begin to understand what he was holding. He came nearer, taking

27

the papers and showing them to him. "It's working out all right . . . look!" And he pointed to a calculation. "I just need a bit more computer time, that's all . . ."

"Computer? What computer's that?"

"One at school."

"And do they know you're using it for this?"

"They know nowt!"

Mr Smith sat on the edge of the bed. "They're not the only ones," he murmured.

"And I'm not telling them!" Martin looked down at his father. "And neither are you, Dad."

"But why not? Why make such a mystery of it? If what you're telling me's right, then, you're . . ." he couldn't finish the sentence—he had thought he knew his younger son, but that was no longer true.

"It's for me, just *me*."

His father felt very tired, as if he'd been running for a long time. "I don't get it. You could have told your Mam . . . me. And your teachers . . . surely they could have helped you . . . "

"That maths teacher? Him? Help *me*?" He turned away, and when he spoke again, his voice was so low that his father could hardly hear him: "I hate him, Dad. I do. I hate him!"

His father was shocked by his bitterness. "You shouldn't hate anyone, son," he said.

"Sneering! Grinning! Making a joke of it!"

"He didn't know!" his father cried. "If you'd told him!"

"Not about me, Dad!" Martin shouted back. "I'm not on about me! That doesn't matter! It's the thing itself: it's maths! That's why I hate him."

His father spread his hands, helplessly. Martin saw his pain, but didn't know how to help—he hadn't any words that would express what he thought.

"So now you know why I've kept it secret. I had to. For there's no one to tell. If I tried, I'd be singing a song to deaf folk."

"Me?" his father asked.

"No. Not you—but if I told you, then I'd be telling them. Then Evans would know." He was silent for a moment, rolling the bundle of papers into a tight tube. "He never once said that maths was beautiful. Not once, in three years. He's blind and stupid and ignorant and trampling. Squashing . . . making mud out of everything. Give *him* these!" And he shoved the papers towards his father. "Flowers to an ape!"

Mr Smith sat, elbows on knees, hands clenched, looking down at the floor.

"I thought I knew you," he said, "but you're away from me. Miles away."

Martin sat next to him. "I'm sorry, Dad."

"Aye . . . well." He looked at his son. "Will you let me tell your Mam?"

"No. Not yet."

"She'll have to know some time."

"Just give me a bit of space, will you?"

His father stood up. "Yes. Of course. Much as you like." He walked to the doorway, then turned to Martin. "One thing," he said, "that Headmaster. I knew he was up the blooming spout . . . and all the rest of them too. But listen, son . . . if you keep owt in the dark long enough . . . it dies."

# THREE

Before they went to bed, the Smiths always had some cheese on cream crackers and a cup of cocoa. It was a time for talking, with the television off, a time when they told each other what they'd been doing during the day and made their plans for the future.

Tonight, Mrs Smith wanted to talk about holidays. She'd been to the travel agent, collected a big pile of brochures, but no one seemed interested. Martin sat silent in the corner, his Dad kept looking at him as if the lad were ill or something, and Barry was in a bad mood.

After a while she gave up trying, gathered up the brochures, put them on the bottom shelf of the bookcase with the old magazines, and went to bed. Something was upsetting them, she knew that, but, whatever it was, sooner or later they would tell her. They always had, and she trusted them.

It'll be something to do with our Martin, she thought, as she drifted off to sleep.

All through the next long day the thought of Barry and his father kept coming back into Martin's mind. Yesterday he'd had a problem, because of the unknown eavesdropper on his computer: now he had a crisis, and very little time in which to resolve it.

As usual, Martin could find some refuge from his worries

in mathematics, and he forced his mind into trying to develop a new theory. He managed to construct a new pattern of thoughts and, at any other time, he would have been excited by it. It was adventurous and dynamic, and would, if it worked, be a tremendous short cut in his work.

Yet now, as he sat in front of the computer, he hadn't his normal enthusiasm for testing it out. He had a sense of foreboding—of his never being able to work at this control panel again.

He tapped out the opening proposition slowly, and left it for a time, waiting for the stranger to make some comment. But nothing appeared. With a shrug of his shoulders he went on to the next statement, but there was still no reply. Perversely, he was annoyed at this—he felt like an actor playing to an empty theatre.

He looked back over what he had done, carefully checking the processes on the screen and noticed, with some irritation, that there was a flaw in the reasoning. How significant it was he wasn't quite sure, but it would have to be checked out. He cleared the screen and went back to the beginning, then tried a different route, but the same error tripped him up. Once more the screen was wiped, and now he wasn't thinking of Barry, of his father or of the stranger: his life was in those figures and they *had* to come right. But they resisted, couldn't be shaped.

Another attempt had to be made, and all his concentration was in it, but it still wouldn't work. He was filled with despair and a sense of disgust that covered the computer, the room, but, more than any of these, himself.

For who was he? A scruffy kid, disliked by everyone, who could do clever tricks with sums. And what was that? Some kids could do handstands, some could beat everyone hollow in the hundred metres. So what was the difference? What was so marvellous about him that he had to hold close to his little gift as if it were a secret of God?

He'd got a puzzle or two that would do to show off with in a rainy play time. And that was all.

He got up, knowing by the cramp in his leg that he'd been sitting for a long time, and switched the computer off. He'd be late home again, but tonight it didn't matter. He would tell them everything and then have done with it.

He put the chair on the bench and climbed up. It was as he was pushing the ceiling panel that he thought that he heard a noise in the room behind him. Scarcely daring to look, he let the panel drop back into place and then slowly turned round.

He was right. Someone was there: a man, shadowed by the sunlight of the corridor, standing in the open doorway. Now it really was all over, and no choosing to be done.

The man didn't say anything, but just looked at him, not frowning, not smiling.

Martin felt both frightened and stupid, standing up there on his chair. He got down and jumped from the bench.

At last the man spoke. "What's your name then?"

"Smith."

"Oh yes?" It was obvious that he wasn't believing him.

"Martin Smith." The stranger lifted an eyebrow. "I'm Barry Smith's brother."

"And what form are you in?"

"IVв, sir."

"And what are you doing here, then?"

Martin didn't know what to say, and cast round in his mind for a way out. Perhaps he could get away with saying that it had all been some sort of dare, put on him by the other kids . . . but no—who'd back *him* up in an alibi?

"I just wanted to see how the computer worked, sir."

"Did you now? But you were in here last night as well, weren't you? And the night before . . . ?"

"No, sir—I wasn't, sir—"

"*I saw you*! So what's the point in lying to me?"

Martin kept quiet after that, and wondered what they did to you for breaking and entering a computer room.

The man walked over to the machine and switched it on, then turned to Martin. "I don't mind boys using this equipment . . . if it's to some purpose. So, let's see, shall we?"

He dotted out a series of figures on the screen, then looked at Martin. "Right," he said, "get on with that lot."

Martin sat at the computer, looked at the figures and couldn't believe what he was seeing: they were the last sequences from his work of the night before.

He turned to face the man: "You teach here, sir?"

"I'm a teacher . . . yes." He nodded towards the computer: "You're wasting time."

Martin put his hands on the keys, but his mind was racing away from the calculations. This man, whoever he was, was the same man who had been sharing his thinking, putting those messages through the computer: but who was he? *Who was he?*

"Come on!" The man's voice now was hard, forceful.

Martin didn't look at him as he said: "I've tried one way forward from that—it didn't lead anywhere."

"Try another way, then. And we haven't much time."

So he began to work, slowly at first and then with gathering speed. It was something, after all, to put right the nonsense of the earlier attempt, for he could see now a new path forward . . . and it seemed to be good.

He reached a conclusion and rested his hands in his lap, not turning round. He could sense that the man had come nearer and that he was now looking over his shoulder.

"That's as far as I want to go for now," Martin said.

"Of course," the man replied, not showing any emotion in his voice.

"You going to report me to the Headmaster, then?"

"I shall have to tell him something, yes."

"You said—"

"I know what I said!"

There was a silence. Martin switched the computer off.

Still the stranger didn't say anything. Martin heard him walk across the room, take the chair off the table. Then he spoke. "Turn round, Martin: let's have a look at you."

Martin did as he was told.

"Do you know how good you are at maths?"

Martin shrugged.

"But no one else knows. Do they?"

"No. My Dad, my brother . . . a little bit. Not everything."

"Why? Why the secrecy?"

"Because no one would understand, they'd just think I was some sort of freak. They don't know about maths. *No one!*"

"They?"

"Teachers . . . other kids."

"I'm a teacher and *I* understand . . . or partly. My mind doesn't go as far as yours . . ."

"I know that . . ." Martin glanced over his shoulder at the computer. "Last night . . . it *was* you, wasn't it?"

The man nodded. "My name's John Doll," he said. "I run a small private school for exceptionally gifted children in the sciences. I think that I ought to have a chat with you and your parents. Don't you?"

*

When Barry came in from his jogging he could hear voices in the front room, and found Martin in the kitchen, putting the best tea-cups on a tray.

"Who's in with Mam and Dad, then?" he asked.

"Headmaster of some school."

"What's he want?"

"*I* don't know, do I?"

"To do with you, though, isn't it?"

Martin nodded. "Perhaps. Here, give us a hand with this lot, Barry, I can't find the sugar bowl." When Barry was near to him, he added in a low voice: "He reckons to run some sort of place for bright kids."

"Oh aye?"

"He might want me to go . . ."

"You're kidding!"

"I'm not . . . it's for maths, sciences."

"And you . . . ?"

"Yes."

"Blimey!"

"Anyway," Martin grinned, "I'd best take this lot in. I reckon they wanted to talk about me behind my back." He squeezed past his brother, carefully balancing the big tea tray.

"Eh!" Barry shouted, as Martin was in the hallway.

"What?"

"This school . . . what do you reckon?"

"Don't know."

"Well, listen, our kid: you needn't go, you know, if you don't want to . . ."

"Right! And thanks, Barry . . ."

He shouldered the front-room door open.

Martin put the tray down on the coffee table by his Mam's chair. She began to pour the tea; delicately, fingers of her left hand lightly holding on to the tea-pot lid.

"Sugar, Mr Doll?"

Martin gave a slight smile, loving her for trying so hard for him and putting on her posh voice.

"No, thanks."

She passed him his tea. "I didn't know that you could do that with computers . . . plug in to someone else's machine."

"Oh yes . . . and this friend of mine at the university lets me play about with their set up whenever I'm up here. Of course, it was just by chance that I picked up what Martin was doing. We don't normally discover our talent like that—usually parents or schools get in touch with us . . ."

"And our Martin . . . he's really clever . . . as clever as the other children at your school?"

"Yes. I think so. And he knows it . . . don't you, Martin?"

"I'm different. I don't know any more than that," Martin replied, looking down at the carpet.

"All this . . . it's come as a bit of a shock to us, hasn't it, love?" She looked across at her husband.

"It certainly has." He glanced at Martin, who lifted his head. But Dad was straight-faced, giving nothing away.

"Why did you never let on to us, Martin?" she asked, the hurt showing in her voice.

"Mrs Smith," Doll murmured, "it's the most natural thing in the world for a boy like Martin to keep a gift like that to himself: and it is, I know, deeply hurtful to those near to him. Einstein, for instance, and Froelich . . ."

"You're not telling us that he's like them!" she cried. "Not our Martin!"

"He may be. You have to face that. But, certainly, they were both expelled by their schools, their genius undetected."

Mrs Smith looked at Martin, as though seeing a different

36

person. Mr Smith concentrated on filling his pipe, but his hands were trembling.

At last Mrs Smith spoke: "This school of yours . . . what do you call it?"

"Falconleigh."

"He'd be properly looked after there?"

"Given every attention, I promise you, and every encouragement. He'd have his own room—everything he needed."

"I don't want to stand in the lad's way," Mr Smith said, "but the fact is, we're not rich folk." He looked round the small room. "Well, you can see . . ."

Doll interrupted him: "There's no question of your having to pay anything. For Martin it will be absolutely free."

"Money must come from somewhere . . ."

"Right—and in our case it comes from the Icarus Foundation."

"That's a sort of charity?"

"Set up by an American millionaire who has chosen to remain anonymous. He wanted to use his money to encourage those few brilliant children in countries all over the world who wouldn't get this opportunity any other way . . ."

"They're all over the world, then, these schools?" Mr Smith asked.

"Oh yes."

"Looks like it's up to you then, son," his father said. "We won't push you either way . . ."

Martin didn't speak, but sat, twisting his watch round and round his wrist.

"What do you think, love?" his Mam asked.

"I don't want to leave home," Martin muttered.

"Or that school of yours?" Doll asked.

"I don't want to go back there. Ever."

"He's quite wrongly placed there," Doll said, an edge of anger in his voice. "Fish out of water! I can't emphasise that too much."

"I see that," Mr Smith said.

Mrs Smith put a hand on Martin's shoulder. "There'll be the holidays, Martin."

"Of course there will," Doll added. "Mind you, I should say, here and now, that most of our pupils don't bother with them too much. Once they get into the swing of the work they hate to break off for anything."

"I wouldn't like . . ." Mrs Smith started to say, but Doll cut in:

"Your boy is not like other boys, Mrs Smith. He's been given great gifts; and, in return for these, great demands will be made of him . . . and of you. The question is . . . are you prepared to pay?"

None of them had noticed Barry come into the room. When he spoke, they turned quickly towards him, as if they'd been surprised in a guilty secret.

"Why rush him? What's the hurry?" he asked.

Martin stood up and looked across at him. "No," he said, "it might as well be now."

"Don't make a mistake," Barry warned.

Martin shook his head. "It's all right. Really."

"Suit yourself. You know best."

"Well?" Doll asked.

Martin looked down at his parents. "I'm sorry, Mam . . . Dad . . . but I think I'll have to go."

"You're doing right, son, I know that," his father said.

His mother nodded in agreement, then she turned to Doll. "This school—Falconleigh . . . I'd like to see it before he goes. Can I do that?"

"Of course: I'll enjoy showing you round, and your

husband too, naturally. We're very proud of the place, you know. . . ."

*

It wasn't until morning break that the Headmaster got the chance of a word with Mr Evans. He saw him in the playground, shouting at some child in the first year. He pushed his window up and called to him across the din of the crowd.

"Mr Evans! Have you a moment?"

Evans came running across. "Stupid lad, that," he smiled.

The Headmaster didn't smile back, so Evans quickly put on a serious face.

"Martin Smith," the Headmaster said.

"He's not in today, missed my maths class, first period. I always thought that truanting would be the next step for that one."

"No. He wasn't in. Nor will he be. It seems that we've lost him."

"Thank God for that!"

"Some sort of special school, I believe."

"About all he's fit for, I'd say, wouldn't you, Headmaster?"

"Very probably: this is, you see, a school for the encouragement of brilliant children. It seems that Master Smith is one such."

"*Smith?*" Evans cried, his voice rising to an unbelieving screech. "We are talking about the same lad? Scruffy, idle object in IVв?"

"The same. I'm very much afraid that you've allowed the brightest pupil that this school has ever possessed to slip unremarked through our fingers."

"It's a joke, Headmaster! It has to be! He's *thick*!"

"So you have said, on many occasions. Others, more

39

perceptive perhaps, seem to differ. The word 'genius' has been bandied about in connection with young Smith."

"Good God!"

"Quite so," the Headmaster said, and closed the window.

# FOUR

Ten days later Martin sat in the luxury of Doll's car and watched the unfamiliar flat countryside flash by. He felt uncomfortable, hot and itchy in his new clothes, as if he were starting with a heavy cold.

"There in a couple of minutes," Doll said.

"Right, sir," Martin replied, dutifully.

"Look—I've told you before—don't call me 'sir'! Don't call anybody 'sir'. Know your own worth!"

"It takes a bit of getting used to, that's all."

"You soon will, though . . ."

After that they didn't speak, until Doll slowed down to turn into a driveway between heavy gateposts. On one of them Martin saw a sign which read: FALCONLEIGH SCHOOL. MAINTAINED BY THE ICARUS FOUNDATION.

"This is it," Doll said. "All right?"

It was more than all right, Martin thought. The drive stretched ahead, gently rising and falling towards the biggest house he'd ever seen, its warm-coloured stone glowing in the sunlight. His Mam had gone on and on about the place, telling everyone how marvellous it was, and he'd thought that she was exaggerating, trying to cheer him up against leaving home, but, if anything, she hadn't done it justice.

"Of course, what you're seeing now is the original building, the new labs and whatnot are round the back."

The car slowed to a halt by a tall flight of stone steps, at the top of which there was a pillared archway. Martin got out and locked around, sniffing the different, fresher air, while Doll opened up the boot of his car and swung the suitcases out. "Grief!" he shouted, as he picked up one of Martin's. "What have you got in here? Rocks?"

"All my Aunties bought me something. They said it would be cold down here."

"Well, by the weight of this, you shouldn't feel it! Here you are, then."

Martin took the case and looked up the steps. He felt very nervous now.

"In you go, then! Don't hang about."

From inside the school came the clamour of a deep-toned gong.

"Good! That's the supper gong: we're just in time."

Martin started to climb the steps, watched by Doll.

"And, Martin . . ."

"Yes?"

"Welcome to Falconleigh . . ."

Once through the doors, Martin was even more impressed. He'd expected something like a grander version of the entrance hall at the comprehensive, but what he saw now had nothing to do with that at all. A fire in a massive grate was crackling through a pile of logs and, on either side of it, deep cushioned, chintz-covered easy chairs were handily placed for rest and relaxation. Gilt-framed portraits lined the oak-panelled walls and, in one corner, a brass-faced grandfather clock delicately ticked away the moments. There was no sound of crowding kids or shouting teachers and, instead of the hard clatter of feet on asphalt, there was the warm luxury of deep carpeting.

Doll stood behind him. "It is beautiful, isn't it?"

Martin nodded, lost for words.

"Let's hope that you like the food as much as the décor. Leave your things there, for now. We'll go and eat."

Doll led the way through a columned doorway into a long corridor. The thick carpeting stretched ahead of them, and through the diamond-paned windows on his left Martin caught glimpses of the soft and brilliant lushness of the school grounds. "My room's first on your right," Doll said.

"All this part we're in now . . . it's out of bounds, I suppose?"

"Practically nothing in the building's out of bounds. You *live* here now, Martin: it's your home."

"You mean I could go and sit in those chairs—by the fire?"

"If you wanted to, of course!"

"Wow!"

Doll grinned and pushed open a carved oak door on their right. "This is the dining-room: we call it the refectory, or the 'ref'."

The refectory reminded Martin of a picture he'd once seen in a history book of a monastery dining-room. Polished oak tables surrounded the walls, with a further long table on a raised platform at the far end of the room. Children sat on benches, their backs to the walls, apart from a few of the older ones who sat with adults at the high table. He guessed that the adults must be teachers, but, from the way in which they were smiling at him, as if they were pleased to see him, they weren't like any teachers *he'd* ever known.

At one side of the platform a small girl was reading aloud from a large book on a stand: from what he could hear it was a learned treatise on chemistry. Some of the children were listening to this while they ate, others had headphones on, and the rest had books of their own, propped up on bookrests in front of their plates.

Doll let him look round for a moment and then, putting his finger to his lips, signalling him to silence, indicated a place for him at the lower end of the table on the right-hand side of the room.

He slid into his space, alongside a blonde girl of about fifteen who totally ignored him and went on absent-mindedly forking food into her mouth and reading a book. Not that any more attention was paid to Doll, who went into his place at the high table equally unnoticed.

A white-coated waiter stood in front of Martin, holding a steaming tureen of soup, and nodding enquiringly at the bowl before him. Martin nodded enthusiastically back, and the waiter ladled the soup out. The first taste of this was a bit of a shock: he didn't know that you could make soup out of fish, but the taste was nice enough.

The rest of the meal passed in the same way: strange but delicious food given as much attention as if it had been porridge.

When everyone had finished eating, Doll got to his feet and banged on the table with a small silver hammer. The reader stopped reading, the kids with headphones on took them off, and those who'd been reading closed their books. Everyone stood up. Martin expected grace, and put on a face for it, and, indeed, it was a grace—of a sort.

"We give thanks," Doll intoned, "to our benefactors in the Icarus Foundation, whose generosity makes this school possible: and we thank those men and women of science throughout the ages whose thought and labours give us light, warmth and food."

Everyone sat down again and Doll smiled round, winking in a friendly way to Martin, then called out, "Discussion!"

44

Martin's blonde neighbour turned to him, and it was the first time he'd been able to have a proper look at her, not liking to stare before. She was certainly very beautiful in a cold, remote, kind of way.

"Subject?" she asked, sharply.

"What . . . ?"

"Your work?"

"Maths—wandering off into physics."

She sighed, and gave him a doubting look. "I do hope that doesn't mean that you're a *dabbler*."

"So do I." He was a bit annoyed at the vigour with which these questions were being put.

"I'm biology," she said, clearly not caring as to whether or not this information was of any interest to him.

"That's good."

He looked round the room. Nearly all the other kids were talking to their neighbours, and most seemed to be having happier conversations than he was. Perhaps he'd be able to change places with someone for the next meal.

"Shall I always sit here, in the same place?" he asked.

She nodded. "As new kids come and others go we'll move up, and in our last year we'll sit up there." She waved a hand in the direction of the high table.

Martin groaned inwardly. "Then we'd best get to know each other," he said.

"It isn't necessary," she replied.

"Maybe not—but if I'm sitting next to you for four more years it'd be a help if I knew your name!"

She leant closer to him. "Look: we don't have particular chums here."

Martin's temper snapped; he'd got away from one lot of rotten kids only to land up with this nutter. "I wasn't asking you to flamin' well marry me; I only asked your name!"

She smiled slightly. "So long as you're quite clear as to

45

the ground rules. I'm Sue Kleiner."

Martin nodded—he'd got that far, at least. "Thanks. I'm Martin Smith."

She looked away from him; it looked as if she'd run out of things to say, and he was in no mood to get the conversation going again. Then, suddenly, she said: "I expect you're jolly glad to be here."

An hour ago he had been—now he wasn't quite so sure.

"Tell you better at the end of term."

"Ah. We don't have those."

"What?"

"Terms . . . didn't they tell you?"

He shook his head. "Something about holidays not being compulsory . . ."

"Not compulsory? They're just *not*. We don't have them. Which is good."

"Is it?"

"Of course; and if you don't think so, you shouldn't be here."

"I see."

"Anyway . . . home's not a patch on Falconleigh."

"That depends on your home: mine's all right."

"You'll see," she said, "once you get into your work."

"Hope you're right."

"Now," she said, firmly, "I have to talk to my other neighbour."

"That leaves me a bit one-sided."

She thought about this for a moment.

"You could cross over and talk to him," she said, indicating a boy on the opposite table. "Mind you, he hasn't spoken to anyone except his tutor for the last eighteen months."

"Thanks a bundle," he muttered. Then he remembered something as she was turning away from him, and tugged at her sleeve. "You haven't told me what sort of work *you're* doing . . . I mean, biology's a pretty big subject."

"Sorry," she replied, "but we don't discuss details."

"Why not?"

"Because if we did it would waste energy and discourage invention. If you don't believe me you can ask Jacko."

"Who's he?"

She nodded towards John Doll, then turned away from Martin to talk with the lad on her other side, a boy with a nineteen-sixties hair cut and a crumpled bomber jacket.

Feeling to be a bit of a spare part, Martin left his place and walked over to Doll.

"Smashing meal, Mr Doll—thanks very much."

"Glad you liked it! Chef tries his best, but he's wasting his time with most of them here. And . . . by the way, you're still being a bit formal. Most kids call me John, or Jack or Jacko. Or 'it'. Take your pick." He put his hand on the shoulder of a younger man, sitting on his left. "And I don't think you've met Peter Farley. He's your tutor."

Farley grinned at Martin. "How do you do, sir," he said.

"Just a minute," Martin said. "He called me 'sir', but *you* said . . ."

"Quite right: so I did. This is the Falconleigh way, you see. You call him Farley, because that's his surname. He calls you 'sir' because, in matters of the mind, which is what, after all, we're concerned with here, you're his superior. OK?"

"But . . . he's my teacher . . ."

"Sort of," Farley nodded.

"Now don't get me wrong," Doll added. "Farley here is a quite splendid chap—First Class Honours degree in maths and all that sort of thing—but if he could actually *teach* you anything, then we'd be wasting our money in bringing you here. In fact, you'll probably be teaching him. Ergo: he calls you 'sir'."

"If I teach him . . . who teaches me?" Martin asked. "And how am I supposed to learn anything?"

"Same way as you've managed up to now," Doll said, "but with a great deal more stimulus and a bit more comfort." He saw Martin's puzzled frown and smiled, putting a hand reassuringly on his arm. "You'll see: it'll all work out. *And stop worrying*: you'll have a fine time . . . won't he, Peter?"

"Do our best in that direction," Farley said.

Doll looked over Martin's head at the rest of the room, stood up and banged on the table again with his silver hammer. "Right!" he shouted. "Chat show's over. And, if it's of any interest to anyone, we're showing an incredibly boring old Laurel and Hardy film in Recreation Two. It's the one about the stairs and the piano." There was an outburst of cheering and table banging at this. "So you can take your coffee in there if you like."

All the children got up and moved towards the door, jostling and pushing as they went. Doll turned back to Martin and Farley.

"We'll take a walk, shall we?" he said, shouting above the row.

"All right with you, sir?" Farley asked.

"Fine . . . fine . . ." Martin replied, not knowing what else to say.

"Good," Doll cried, trying to push his way through the crowd. "You could get killed in this place, I'm telling you . . ."

Martin followed the other two up a staircase and along another carpeted corridor, until Farley opened a door and switched on the light. "This is your room, sir," he said to Martin.

At first sight it was rather disappointing. To start with, it was completely empty; not even a carpet on the floor. Then it bore too obviously the signs of its last occupant—a tea stain on the window ledge, and lighter patches on the walls where posters had been pinned. Martin's face showed what he felt, and Doll read his thoughts.

"Don't let it put you off," he said. "This is only the shell: what happens next is up to you. Got the catalogue, Peter?" Farley handed him a large loose-leaf book that he had been carrying under his arm since they left the refectory. "Now," Doll went on, "take a squint at this—it's got pictures of all the furniture and whatnot that we carry in stock. Choose what you want and it'll be in by lunchtime tomorrow. Same with the painting of the walls and your curtains, carpets and so on. Entirely up to you."

Martin stood by the window and looked out at the view. In front of him, but at some distance, there were the roofs of a group of huts; those must be, he thought, the extra labs that Doll had told him of, but beyond them were the woods and fields of the estate. He looked down at the stain on the window ledge.

"Kid who had this room before . . . what happened to him?" he asked.

"Do you know, I really can't say what he's doing now," Doll replied. "Can you, Peter?"

"'Fraid not," Farley said. "We seem to have lost touch, rather."

"I do know that he was something of a disappointment to us," Doll added. "Great shame. However, I'm sure that nothing like that's going to happen in your case, young Smith. Now: if you'll excuse me, I'd better go and make absolutely sure that they've fixed up the guest room for you . . . just for tonight, you understand."

Martin walked over to the right-hand wall of the room

and looked at a panel of lights and switches that was placed there.

"What's this?' he asked.

"Farley will explain all that to you. All right?"

"Yeah . . . great."

"It is indeed. See you at breakfast." And, whistling cheerfully, he went out of the room.

"He sounds happy," Farley smiled.

"Not surprised—place like this! I never heard of a school like it!"

"There isn't a school like Falconleigh, sir."

"You're not kidding." Martin turned to the panel. "About this lot . . ."

"It's really quite simple, sir, it's here to give you whatever you want when you want it. Look, if you don't feel like going to the ref for breakfast, you flick this switch . . . and . . ." As he pressed the switch a green light came on over it and, within a few seconds, a voice was heard from a small speaker in the corner of the panel.

"Kitchens here, sir: did you want something?"

Farley pressed another switch and said: "No, it's all right, just testing." He turned to Martin: "Unless you felt like . . . ?"

"No," Martin said, "I'm fine, thanks."

Farley turned the speaker off. "Whatever you fancy they'll try and get you, and it's a twenty-four hour service."

"Egg and chips at three in the morning?"

"Actually, they'd think that that was a very ordinary and boring sort of request. Kids here try to catch them out —plovers' eggs, smoked salmon, that sort of thing." He pointed to another switch on the panel. "This one's for sick bay, if you're not feeling so good."

"After the egg and chips?"

"Probably . . . and this last one connects you directly to

me or John Doll. There's always someone on call if you want to talk about your work. Not that either of us would be able to help, like as not, but sometimes it's good to talk."

"Speaking of work, when do I start?"

"First thing tomorrow . . . if that's all right, sir."

"Fine. Sooner the better, I suppose."

"Good. Now, what happens is that I bring you a problem to solve. We call these problems 'challenges'. You can take as long as you like about doing it, and if you need any equipment—anything at all—to meet the challenge, you see me and I get it for you."

"How will I know if I've got the right answer?"

Farley smiled. "Haven't a clue: but we hope that *you* will know. Anyway, that's for tomorrow. You must be absolutely flaked so, if you're ready, I'll take you to the guest room." He walked over to the door, politely holding it open so that Martin could go out first. "By the way . . . have you decided on a colour for this room?" he asked, as Martin passed him.

"Grey."

"All over?"

"The lot."

"Very good, sir: I'll let the painters know straight away."

\*

Martin was exhausted by all the events of the day, and fell asleep in no time but, two hundred miles further north, his brother Barry was having a very restless night. After a couple of hours he got up, went downstairs and put a pan of milk on the cooker. His Mam heard him and shouted down, "Is that you, Barry?"

"No, it's Burglar Bill and I'm robbing you something rotten!" he shouted back. After that she was quiet. He got a cup down from the shelf and noticed that Martin's mug had been put away. He stood, thinking about this, turning his

51

cup in his hand. To his surprise he was missing the little perisher.

He made his drink and took it back to bed, thinking about the strangeness of human nature. How can you miss a nuisance?

# FIVE

Martin had slept so soundly that he was rather late for breakfast, but, as he looked round the ref, he saw that most of the kids were going to be even later, for places were set but unoccupied. Sue, however, was there, a plate of bacon and eggs untouched in front of her. She wasn't even looking at it, but staring straight ahead, chin cupped in her hands.

The waiter placed a menu card in front of him, then while he was waiting for Martin to order, he glanced across at Sue's plate. "Finished, miss?" he asked. But her only reply was to nod absent-mindedly. He turned to Martin. "Ready to order, sir?"

"Double bacon and eggs, please, a couple of sausages and four rounds of toast."

The waiter showed no surprise at this order. "Tea or coffee, sir?"

"Coffee, please."

"Very good, sir." And the waiter hurried away, carrying Sue's breakfast.

Martin was determined to try again with this odd girl. After all, why not? The sun was shining, life was good and breakfast was coming.

"Hi!" he said, but got no response. Try once more. "Bet you don't get service like this in a posh hotel, no matter how much you paid. We stayed in a nice place in Spain on our holidays last year, but it wasn't a patch on this . . ."

She came out of her trance and noticed that he was there. "What did you say?"

"Food . . . it's good."

She turned away again. "We don't *have* to talk to people, you know, not at breakfast."

"Sorry for breathing," he said, giving up.

"It's a rule. Talking's for supper time. Breakfast's for thinking."

"*I* didn't know, did I? I'm the new boy here, remember."

At that the waiter came back, with a huge plate of food for Martin.

"Thanks . . . that's smashing," Martin said.

Sue turned to him again and, like last night, there was that sudden smile. "I'm sorry . . . I was very rude. I shouldn't have snapped at you."

Martin nodded his acceptance of her apology: he couldn't do more than that with a mouthful of toast and bacon. She saw the pile of food on his plate and her eyes went wide.

"Goodness! Did you eat as much as that at home?"

"Do you know how much bacon costs? My Mam would have killed us! No . . . weekdays I'd grab a piece of toast and run; much as I had time for. My Dad made us a big fry up on Sundays, though."

The doors banged open and John Doll came in, a pile of newspapers under his arm. He looked across at them and gave an appreciative whistle at the sight of Martin's plate.

"Nothing wrong with your appetite, anyway!" he called.

"I'm still waiting for mine," Sue shouted.

"Sorry about that," and he clicked his fingers for the waiter. "What would you like? Same as him?"

"What *do* you think I am? Half that lot would be too

much." Doll passed her order on to the waiter, then turned back to Martin. "Chosen your furniture yet?"

"Yes . . . got the catalogue here . . . I've ticked what I want." And he gave the book to Doll, who quickly flicked through it, noting his choices.

"No problem. It'll be there by lunchtime. The decorators are in now, I believe . . . and I've had your luggage moved across." He was silent for a moment, looking thoughtfully at Martin. Then: "None of my business, I suppose . . . but what made you fetch a pair of binoculars?"

Martin was startled: he'd had the glasses out of his case last night, making sure that they were all right . . . but he could swear he'd put them back. Still—maybe he was mistaken. "It's my hobby—bird-watching."

Doll nodded. "That's fine. That's really good. Thing is though, I fancy you won't have much time for hobbies once you get into your work."

"Oh?"

"Shouldn't have thought so . . ."

\*

For a couple of hours after breakfast Martin worked on the challenge that Farley had given him. It was very straight-forward and he'd found himself yawning as he finished it. He hoped that they'd find him something a bit livelier than that next time. He looked at his watch and saw that he was too late for coffee and an hour too early for lunch. But the sun was shining in through the windows, and there were the grounds to explore, so he piled his papers together on the library table, scribbled a note for Farley, and tip-toed out.

It was two hundred years since the grounds of Falcon-leigh had been laid out; and it had taken all of that time to bring them to their present glory. The house was built on a slight hill, and every prospect, from every window of the great house, had been designed as a thing of beauty in itself and as part of the whole grand design.

Martin stood on the top step of the house and was moved by what he saw. The turnings of the stream that fell through the woods and the perfect symmetry of the lake into which it flowed spoke to him as a mathematician and as a creator.

He walked down the steps and across the grass, feeling as if he had become part of a sublime painting, and as if, for the first time in his life, he was free.

He heard a cry behind him and turned, disappointed that his walk was going to be spoiled by company. It was Farley, walking fast to catch up with him.

"Taking a walk, sir?" Farley panted. "Bit of exercise?"

"Thought I might as well," Martin replied, hoping that the man would leave him.

"What about your work, though? Wouldn't it be better to get that out of the way first?"

"That kid's puzzle you gave me? Finished!"

"You sure, sir?"

"Certain. It's on a table in the library. You'd best go and pick it up, Farley. I'd hate it to go missing."

"Yes indeed," Farley said, his eyes narrowing a little. It hadn't taken this one long to pick up the Falconleigh style!

"And after dinn—" Martin started to say, then corrected himself—"lunch, I think I'll do a bit of bird-watching: unless you've got another challenge ready for me?"

"We can't set challenges that fast . . . especially at the level you seem to be operating at . . ."

"That's what I thought."

"All the same . . . I wouldn't make any definite plans, sir . . . we may find something else for you to do . . ."

"That would be good," Martin said, not really thinking about it as he strode towards the lake.

Lunch was the best meal he'd had at Falconleigh. The

food was, as before, superb, but, more than that, the atmosphere in the ref was friendly and relaxed. Even Sue was easier to talk to—he still wouldn't describe her as being friendly, but she was at least interested in what he was saying and putting her own two penn'orth in. It was only when he tried to find out something about herself that she clammed up, but by that time it didn't matter too much, they'd lingered for half an hour over their coffee, and Martin felt that he could put up with her quite easily for the next few years.

He soon found a fairly decent hide, just outside the woodland, and settled down to wait. It was a long wait too. Typical, he thought; this morning, when he hadn't got his glasses, he'd seen at least two birds that he wanted a closer look at and now . . . nothing.

At last, though, his patience was rewarded, and he forgot about his cramp and the fact that the grass was really a bit damp, as a red-necked phalarope floated into view. It was a bird he'd never seen before and though he wasn't interested in ticking off specimens in a note-book, there was a great thrill in seeing a bird for the first time: and the phalarope is a most beautiful bird. Easily it floated on a thermal, rising without effort, wings spread on the warm air, held, wonderful. He was filled with the mystery of it and the grace of its strength, and his spirit flew with it, free, unencumbered.

Then a hand shook his shoulder, so that his glasses slipped from the view. Furious, he threw the glasses down and pushed himself on to his side. It was Sue standing there, face pink with running.

"Couldn't you see what I was doing?" he cried.

"Don't blame me!" she shouted back. "I've been sent to get you!"

"What for?"

"I don't know . . . they want you to play the Game, probably!"

"Who does?"

"Jacko, and your tutor bloke."

"What game's that, then?"

"You'll see. Anyway, hurry up; they don't like being kept waiting." She was already walking quickly back to the school.

"Where's it at, then, this game?" he shouted after her.

"Games Room . . . where else would you expect . . ."

Martin stood in the doorway and looked round the squash court: if that was the game he was expected to play he hadn't the slightest idea of the rules, nor had he any kit. Then he saw Farley, sitting at one side of a plain wooden table in the centre of the space. On the table was a lamp, the sort of thing he'd seen in spy films when the hero was being interrogated. Farley had a book in his lap and was reading it with great concentration, not looking up at Martin.

"You wanted me?" Martin asked. But Farley didn't reply and went on reading. "Something about a game . . ." Farley nodded at this, but his eyes were still on his book. Martin stood for a few more moments, not knowing what to do: then he began to feel angry—he'd better things to do than hang about here waiting for this guy to finish the chapter. He turned to go.

"Where do you think you're off to?" Farley said, and there was no trace of friendliness in his voice now. He sounded colder, more distant than even the hardest of teachers at Martin's other school.

"You didn't seem bothered . . . so I thought . . ."

Farley interrupted him. "Sit down. That chair." And he nodded at the chair on the opposite side of the table.

Martin shrugged his shoulders and walked over to the chair, pointedly moving it a foot or two away from the table before sitting down. Farley went back to his book.

"Shouldn't you be calling me 'sir'?" Martin asked.

"Not here. We're all equal in the Game." And Farley put his book very carefully on the table, marking his place with a slip of paper. Then he looked across the table at Martin.

If that was the way he wanted it, Martin thought, that was the way he could have it. "Fair enough . . . Peter. So, when do we start playing this game, then?"

Farley thought about this for a moment. "Maybe we've already started. What do you think?"

"Maybe *you* have! I don't know. I haven't a clue what we're supposed to be doing."

"We're playing the Game. That's what you've come for; you know that."

Martin grinned. "You should have blown a whistle, then I'd have known."

"You reckon?"

"Told me the rules."

"You like rules?" Farley said, switching the lamp on. It shone straight into Martin's eyes and he smiled again at the crudeness of it. Casually, he tapped the shade so that it shone on Farley.

"Rules? Well, most games have them. They say that's what makes them fun."

Farley adjusted the lamp so that it shone on neither of them. "People invent rules, though. Someone steps out and says, 'No: we'll play it *this* way.' Then you get rules."

Martin sighed. Falconleigh had been too good to be true, and now he'd come to the catch in it—playing stupid games with an idiot.

"So, come on, Smith, you to decide what game we're playing and tell me the rules."

"I'm telling you, it'll never catch on: but still . . . here we

59

go . . ." He looked round the room. "Squash court," he said.

"Could be. So?"

"But we've no . . . rackets? Is that what they call them? Or a ball. So it's not going to be much of a game of squash."

"Shame," Farley said, sarcastically.

Martin ignored the sarcasm: he wanted to keep his temper, having a feeling that Farley was trying to make him lose it. "Not really: I don't think I'd be very good at it."

"Then what sort of game can it be?"

"Has to be competition. Between you and me. No ball . . . nothing. So it's a thinking game."

Farley nodded, very slowly. "Looks like it."

"No paper, pencils. We talk the game."

"Tough on you, I'd have thought. I'd have said that you carried a bit of a handicap there, old sport . . ."

It was hard for Martin to keep his temper: the flick of contempt in Farley's voice had been obvious. He had to hit back, though. " 'Old sport'," he grinned. "Where did you drag that up from?"

"It's only taken us a day to suss you out, Smith," Farley drawled. "That maths master of yours was spot on. You're a Yorkshire yob, aren't you, Smith? A bit of dirt in the gutter."

"Talking about me?" Martin asked, his voice low. " 'cos if you *are*, and the game's called 'insults' . . ."

"You're making the rules, not me, or, more accurately, you're rather pathetically trying . . ."

"I said, if the game's called 'insults' and we're going to swap nasties, I should warn you, Farley, that you're taking on the champ. How else could a kid like me live in the school I've come from?" He waited for a response from Farley, but there was no change in his expression. "Want to carry on?"

"A scrap with rubbish like you doesn't frighten me."

Martin nodded, accepting. "Right," he said, speaking slowly and clearly. "You reckon you're a mathematician. OK? Which means that you've wrapped yourself up cosy in some degree from Cambridge, where no one's had a really original idea since Rutherford—and if anyone had, they'd have all dropped dead with fright at the sight of it. I could buy and sell you at mathematics without breaking into a sweat, old sport."

"So you're a freak. Congratulations."

"Oh no! No freak. I'm what you ought to be . . . and what you'd like to be. You called me a Yorkshire yob, but if you could do half what I can, you'd eat Yorkshire pudding till it came out your ears and stand on the terraces shouting yourself stupid for Leeds United. But you never will. Never. It won't come to you now, will it? Your chance was never really there, but it's gone now. And you know, almost as well as I do, that you're not a mathematician: you're a middle-aged nothing who's fairly competent at doing sums —but a three-quid pocket calculator's better."

Farley got up and Martin thought that he was going to hit him. But he rammed his hands into his pockets and walked away. "So you're different!" he shouted. "But how long do you think that'll last? Kids like you—we've had dozens of 'em here, and do you know what? By the time they're twenty they're burned out! Finished! And I can tell you this for nothing—they're not even much good at doing sums any more! Dead, everything gone!"

Martin wasn't shaken. "Not me," he said, very softly.

Farley came near to him again, leaning over the table. "You sure?"

"Certain sure. I've been given something . . . and it's mine as long as I hold it."

"Taken away from you . . . it could be."

"No way. It'd have to be . . . ." It was as if he was trying to find the right word, but a flicker of fear came into his eyes. Farley saw it and took the advantage.

"What? *What would it have to be?*"

Martin was bending over now, fists clenched between his knees. "Wasting it . . ." he whispered.

"How could you do that?"

There was a long silence before he answered.

"I don't know . . . that's to be learned."

*

At the end of the Games Room was what Martin had thought was a large mirror, but behind it, Doll was leaning forward and watching every move. From his side it was no mirror but a dark window. He was smiling slightly, enjoying the contest. He switched on the microphone that was in front of him, whispered a command into it and sat back. Farley nodded slightly as he received the order in the tiny speaker concealed in his ear.

"Well played, Martin," he said, sitting down again.

Martin looked up at him. "Lousy game," he said.

"Oh, I don't know, anyway, you won."

"Won?"

"Hands down."

"That's nice . . . but what was it for?"

"Me getting to know you, sir: you getting to know me."

"Must be easier ways . . ."

"They reckon not, sir."

Martin got up: he felt very tired. "Can I go now?" he asked.

"You're the boss, sir—any time you like . . ."

Martin needed a breath of air and walked through to the front of the school and out into the grounds, but the sun had gone in and the woods that had been so green and soft an hour ago looked black and threatening now. He shivered against the cold and came back in, walking quickly along the corridor to his room: maybe if he were to do some work it would clear his mind.

But when he opened his door he saw that he had a visitor—John Doll was lounging in the deck chair that he had ordered.

"Like your room," Doll smiled. "Primitive simplicity, I think I'd call it." And, indeed, the room was plainly furnished. Grey walls, grey carpet, a row of cushions along one wall to serve as a bed, a card table and folding chair for a working space, the deck chair that Doll was occupying; these were the total sum of Martin's choices from the range he'd been offered.

"But, I ask myself," Doll went on, "is this severity or instability?"

"What do you mean?"

Doll glanced round the room. "Nothing here to hold you."

"I don't like fuss . . . clutter."

Doll nodded, approvingly. "Good."

"But you're right. I want to go."

Doll expressed no surprise. "Why?"

"I don't like the games you play."

"Then you must find better ones."

"Don't *you* start on that!" Martin said, the anger that he'd felt in the Games Room coming back to him so strongly that his hands started to tremble. "Trying to pretend that I was choosing. It was set up!"

"Come and sit down, Martin," Doll murmured, his voice level and unemotional.

"No thanks!"

"All right. Stay where you are, then. But listen, and try to believe me. All the kids here play that sort of game. It's a battle of wits between fairly witful people, that's all. After a few sessions the kids enjoy it, look forward to it. They know that if we're to work together we've got to get to know each other better than anyone's ever known us before."

"Supposing I said that I don't want to know you . . . and I don't want you to know me . . . ?"

"OK. You can say that now—but in a couple of weeks you won't. It's all for you, Martin . . . You've got to believe that. For you and your gift."

"No."

"It's true," Doll said, walking over to him. "All that I want is to release what's in you. Free your spirit and your mind—let them climb, fly, rise and soar. And if we use science to do that, have you, a scientist, the right to complain?"

Martin walked over to his table and looked out of the window, needing to get away from Doll. His mind was too tired to cope with these arguments, but Doll came after him, standing close behind him, one hand on his shoulder.

"You must trust me, Martin," he said. "You can go, if you want to, of course—this isn't a cage. But do try to remember what you'll be going back to."

Martin half turned towards him, then changed his mind and went back to staring out of the window. Doll took a sheet of paper out of his pocket and leant past him to place it on the table. "While you're thinking about your future, spare a couple of minutes for glancing over that," he said. "It's quite a problem, way beyond me—but of course that goes without saying."

For a time, Martin didn't respond, as if he hadn't heard him. Then he glanced down at the paper. He frowned as he registered the complexity of it. Then he picked it up, biting his lower lip in concentration.

"I think that it's beyond me too."

"Try it . . . see what happens . . ."

Martin shook his head. "No, you see . . . ." He glanced at

64

Doll and realised that even to tell him *why* it was difficult would be impossible. "Who sets these things, anyway?" he asked.

"I don't know . . . someone in Head Office . . . computer, probably."

Martin put the paper back on the table and leant over it, hands gripping tightly at the table sides. Absent-mindedly, he switched the lamp on.

Doll walked out of the room, quietly closing the door.

*

It took him days to come to the end of that problem: never had he had anything so difficult to master. But, at Falconleigh, the path was cleared of all obstacles that could have held him up. Whatever he wanted was provided—books, research papers, computer time. And, as each day passed, he could feel the strength of his mind growing; that which, a month ago, he would have said was impossible, was now taken as part of his daily routine.

And his days had a pattern: the breakfast chat with Sue (who was now almost friendly), then back to his room for work until the waiter crept in with his morning coffee. Ten minutes break for that, then once more at his desk until lunch, which, if the work was flowing fast, he'd take in his room. After lunch he would pick up his binoculars and go to his hide by the edge of the woods. Then back to his room for tea and cakes and work again until supper.

The hide that he had made was good, now. He was sheltered from the worst of the weather, and completely concealed from every side. He was happy, on that bright autumn day: to be there, to be so free and so sure of himself.

A great bird flew into his vision, and his glasses held it, he saw its bright commanding eyes, its scarcely ruffled plumage and the reaching arch of its wings. It came low over him, he put the glasses down—it was too close for him to have need of them. Then it rose up and away, towards the huts at the edge of the school, and held itself there, high, wings scarcely beating. He lifted up his glasses again and, as the bird came into sharp focus, he saw the strong rhythm of it alter. It turned towards him, but its flight was now crippled and maimed: its wings twisted, its head turned in a line of agony and it fell, over and over, all grace blown away and its beauty reduced to a scrap of bone and feather.

For long moments he didn't move, nor did he hear his own cry, and then he ran, over the smooth and well-kept parkland, to where it had fallen. It was there, contorted, eyes open, hard and glassed over, feathers ruffled now by the slight wind that was blowing Martin's hair into his eyes. At first he didn't touch it: the change from its living to this was so terrible to him, but then he carefully picked it up, smoothing its wings open and lifting its head. He took it close to the warmth of his body: but there was no way to breathe life back to it.

Cradling it in his arms, pulling his coat over it, rocking backwards and forwards, Martin silently wept.

# SIX

After a while, he opened his coat, took the bird out, looked long and hard at it and then, gathering some stones from the edge of the wood, carefully buried it.

Then he went back to his room, ordered some tea and drank it, thinking. His room grew dark, but he didn't switch his lamp on. He was quite still, sitting cross-legged on his cushions. From far off, he heard the supper gong and at that he got up, went to the bathroom, scrubbed his hands until they were red and stinging, combed his hair and went to eat.

He was like the other children now, not noticing what he was eating. The reader read, but Martin didn't hear her and, when the meal was done and Doll had said the Falconleigh grace, he still sat, staring straight ahead.

Sue shook his arm and he turned to her. "Well?" she said.

"What . . . ?"

"Is anything the matter? You look terrible."

"No. I'm fine . . ."

"Maybe you should see Matron—she'd give you something."

"Look . . . I've told you . . . I'm all right."

"Suit yourself . . ." And she turned to her other neighbour.

"Sue," he said, "if you've nothing better on tomorrow

afternoon—would you come for a walk with me?"

She considered this for a moment, head on one side. "If you like," she said.

After supper Martin went back to his work like a starving man faced with food. It went well—page after page of notes built up into a pile on his table, and crumpled sheets filled the waste-paper basket. Farley had to knock several times at the door before Martin heard him.

"Come in!" he shouted.

"Hope I'm not disturbing you," Farley said.

"That's a daft thing to say." Martin glanced at his papers. "But I suppose I've nearly finished, so I'll let you off."

"That was quick," Farley said, sitting on one of the cushions.

"I was lucky—it ran right."

"Good."

"Tell you one thing, though: I got a research paper from the library, connected with the stuff I've been doing, and the fellow that wrote it's up the creek."

"Which paper's that, sir?"

"One on the floor by the side of you."

Farley picked the paper up, glanced at the author's name.

"He's a professor . . . Harvard, I think."

"Don't care where he is, he's still miles out. So, get rid of it would you? It's rubbish."

Farley threw the paper into the waste-paper basket. "If you say so . . ." And he got up to go.

"There's something else . . ."

Farley turned towards him. "Yes?"

"Those huts, the ones you can see from this window . . ."

"What about them, sir?"

"Tell me what they're used for."

68

Farley shrugged his shoulders. "Nothing much, in fact they're storerooms—lab equipment, that sort of thing."

Martin shook his head. "No."

"No?"

"I don't think so. A bird flew over them this afternoon. It was killed. And something in one of those huts killed it."

"Come off it," Farley smiled.

"It did. I saw it. And I want to know how. And I want to know why."

Farley's smile had faded now. "In that case, I'll look into it."

Martin returned to his work. It was late to take it on to the next stage, but he knew that he wouldn't sleep easily that night unless he drove himself to exhaustion. He was soon deep into it, so deep that he didn't hear the helicopter coming in low overhead for a landing. John Doll heard it, however, glanced at his watch and strode out of his room, out of the building and towards the landing pad behind the trees. The visitor who was coming would have to be met, have to be given all the courtesies that Falconleigh could offer.

*

The day had promised well, but during lunch the sky had clouded over and now a fine rain was falling. Sue and Martin stood in front of the small heap of stones.

"Just fell?" Sue asked. "Out of the sky?"

He nodded.

"Could be natural, birds do die, you know."

"No. There was nothing wrong with it."

"Best have a look, then. Get the stones shifted and we'll see."

Martin knelt and started to move the stones, but he had only shifted a couple when he felt that there was someone standing behind him. He turned, pulling the hood of his anorak back and saw Catherine Elton, Sue's tutor. She must have come up very quietly, he thought.

"Gave us a fright—creeping up like that!" Sue exclaimed.

"I'm sure I made enough noise, just that you two were so busy . . ." She looked down at the stone that Martin held in his hand. "Lost something, sir? Pen? Watch? Easily done, I know . . ."

"No," Sue said. "He . . ."

But Martin interrupted her. "I've not lost anything."

"Then what . . . ?"

"Just messing on," Martin said, throwing the stone past her and into the bushes.

She looked at him for a moment, then nodded. "I see. Then don't let me stop you—messing on."

"I've finished now. And I'm cold. So I'm going back. Coming, Sue?"

"Yes, if you like," Sue said, her frown showing her puzzlement at his strangeness.

Elton still stood, head on one side, looking at them, waiting for something.

"Anything else you wanted, Elton?" Sue asked.

"No, ma'am."

"Then don't let me keep you," Sue said, her voice crisp and firm like a rich woman ordering a servant about. "I'm sure that you have a lot to do."

"Your challenge, ma'am . . ."

"Will be done in time. I'll see you in my room, after supper."

"As you wish, ma'am." And Elton turned and began to walk away, back to the school, stopping once to look back at them.

Martin shook his head. "Never get used to talking to teachers like that," he said.

"Don't notice it after a bit." She looked down at the remaining stones. "Well?"

"It's gone," he said.

They heard the voice of Elton, shouting from a distance, "Come on, you two!"

"Look!" And Martin kicked the stones aside. "Someone's shifted it."

"Animal? Stoat? Weasel?"

Martin shook his head. "Animal wouldn't have put the stones back."

Sue walked away from him, shoulders hunched, hands in her anorak pockets.

"You don't believe me!" he said. "You don't believe that there ever was a bird!"

"Like you said," she replied, still not looking at him, "it's late and we ought to be getting back . . ."

*

The living-room of Martin's house looked just the same as it had done those weeks ago when he left, except that there was now a big framed photograph of him on the mantel-shelf. His father put the phone down.

"Well?" Mrs Smith asked.

"Same as usual," he replied. "He's keeping very well, but just now he's busy with his work and doesn't want to be disturbed, and they'll get him to ring back when he's finished. I'll wring his perishing neck for him when I get my hands on him, I know that much . . ."

"If he's all right, though . . ."

"Oh, aye . . ."

"Still, I wish he'd get in touch . . ."

Barry had been sitting in a corner of the room, twisting a length of string round and round his hand. He looked towards his mother, frowning. "My half-term starts on Monday," he said.

71

"So . . . ?"

"And there'll be nowt on at school next couple of days . . ."

Mrs Smith nodded; she knew what was in his mind. "And you fancy a bit of a break then . . . ?"

"Aye. I thought I might do a bit of hitch-hiking."

"Far as Norfolk?"

"Maybe . . ."

"Well, give him our love if you see him, and ask if there's anything he wants."

*

When Sue and Martin got back to the school, Farley was waiting for them in the entrance hall. "Could I have a word, sir?" he said to Martin.

Sue took her anorak off and shook it. "Want me too?" she asked.

"No. Just Martin—if you don't mind, ma'am."

"Feel free! I'm off for a cuppa, anyway . . ." And she left them, slamming the door as she went.

"My room?" Martin asked.

"Why not stay here? It's quite comfortable." And Farley stood in front of the fire, warming his hands at the blaze. Martin noticed that they were so thin that the flames glowed through them.

"About that bird . . . and the huts," Farley said.

Martin sat in one of the easy chairs and nodded. "Yes?"

"You know, from time to time we allow one or two of our students whose work demands it to carry out fairly practical tests . . ."

"Like killing things?"

"No. Never that."

"I saw that bird die."

Farley turned to face him. "Impossible. The huts hold nothing but out-of-date equipment. When you told me

72

about this bird I thought that maybe someone was doing something . . . experimental. But they're not. And no one's been in the huts for days." He came nearer to Martin, leaning over him, his hands on the arms of the chair. "Bring me the bird; I'll have one of our biologists look at it. And I'm sure that it died of some illness."

"I can't do that."

"Why not?"

"Because someone's taken it."

Farley straightened up and looked down at him. "Oh, Martin, Martin," he said, his voice full of pity.

"What's that supposed to mean? That I'm soft in the head or something?"

"Of course not . . . but you must see . . . without the wretched bird . . . what can we do?"

*"Someone took it!"*

"Try and rest content with what I've told you: there's nothing at Falconleigh to harm anyone or anything. You've got to believe that . . ."

Martin thought for a moment, then got up out of the chair. "If you say so . . ."

"Not just a question of my saying so: you've got to think so . . ."

*

Martin intended to work in his room, but his mind was so ill at ease that he knew that not even mathematics would clear it. He needed to talk with someone, and he thought longingly of Barry and his Mam and Dad. He wondered whether to try again to ring them up: perhaps this time they would be in, but, then again, how could he make them see that a bird dying was so important? He looked at his watch—an hour to go before supper. He stared dispiritedly out of the corridor windows at the drizzle still clouding the view. There had to be *someone* he could talk it out with; but he didn't know anyone at Falconleigh apart from Sue—and by the look she'd given him he didn't think he'd get much of a welcome there. All the same . . . perhaps . . .

Without hoping for very much he set out to find her room. That took him a long time, since he didn't want to ask anyone for directions, but eventually he came upon it at the end of a long and twisting corridor in the oldest part of the house. Her name was on the door, but underneath this there was another card, this time crudely blocked out with felt-tipped pen: KEEP OUT.

He almost changed his mind at that, then decided to take a chance. He knocked on the door, but there was no response. Perhaps she's out, he thought. Then there was a muffled shout from the room which could have meant anything, but he hoped that it meant "come in", so he opened the door.

What he saw then stopped him where he stood. Where his room was grey and plain, this one was like a Victorian dream of rich plenty. Huge and ornate furniture oppressed the space, and the dim light was filtered through layers of net and vast swagged curtains. The walls were covered with dark flock paper.

"Wow," he said.

Sue was working behind an enormous carved desk, her face lit by an oil lamp. "Didn't you see the notice?" she asked. "I'd have thought that it was clear enough."

"Yes. I did. But I need to talk to someone."

"Can't it wait?"

"I don't think so."

"Then you'd best come in, shut the door and sit down." And she shifted a pile of books off a cushioned cane chair. "Anyway, we're not supposed to go into each other's rooms you know. It's a rule."

"I didn't know."

"Well you do now. So you'd best hurry up."

"All right. Sue . . . that bird . . . I *did* see it, it *did* die and I *did* bury it . . ."

"Look Martin, does it matter? It's only a blooming bird, when all's said and done . . ."

"It was *killed*!" he cried.

"So you keep telling me. But what can *I* do?"

"Peter Farley says that nothing here harmed it."

"Well then he must be right! He'd know . . ." She looked at him, pressed into the shadow of the chair, eyes large and staring in the whiteness of his face. "Listen, Martin . . . and don't take what I'm saying the wrong way . . . there are times when we all work too hard here—it's a sort of Falconleigh disease. When we do, then funny things happen . . ."

"What sort of things?"

"All kinds, daftnesses . . . I've been through it myself and I know. Once I thought I heard my father arguing with Jacko in the hall—when I got there, there was no sign of them. He hadn't been near the place. I'd imagined it."

"So *I* imagined what *I* saw . . . ?"

"I don't know, do I? But it's possible."

He closed his eyes and wondered if this could be true. He had been working hard: pretty well non-stop, and now that he looked back on the day all the events seemed to be like something out of a dream.

"Would you like some tea?" she asked. "There'll still be some in the pot . . . it'll be a bit chill, but . . ."

"Thanks. That'd be good."

She poured him the tea and he looked round the room and noticed a newspaper photograph, crudely torn from the page and pinned on the wall. It was very blurred, but he could make out a lady wearing academic dress being congratulated by a man wearing what looked like a golden teacher's gown and a mortar-board. Behind them there was a seated row of applauding people.

"Who's that?" he asked.

"Mummy picking up another doctorate at some university or other, and that's Daddy behind her, clapping. They take it turn and turn about—sometimes she claps and he gets, then they swap. It's a hobby with them."

"What are they like?"

"Academics. Very brilliant. Surely you've heard of their great book . . . *Patterns of Child-Rearing in Twentieth-Century Britain*?"

He shook his head.

"Amazing!" she went on, her voice becoming more bitter and strident. "People talked about nothing else for at least a week-end. The book, of course, is a total joke . . ."

"Why?"

"Why? *Why*? Look at me for God's sake!"

He was startled by the rawness of her hurt—there was no sign now of the cold and reserved girl he'd first met. "Don't you like them?" he mumbled, embarrassed to be asking such a question.

"Like them? *I don't even know them*! Me as a kid, growing up, parcelled up and sent to this aunt or that cousin. Then summer comes, and it's adventure holiday time, folks! I've had more bloody adventures than Robinson Crusoe!"

"Must have been rotten."

"What do you know about it?"

"Nothing. Except what you've told me. My parents are all right so I can't know, can I?"

"Lucky old you," she snapped. "Drink up your tea and get out, will you . . . I've got work to do . . ."

He stood up. "I'm sorry . . . about your parents."

"Thanks." But she was already at her desk and sorting through her papers. Then she looked up. "And I wouldn't be too smug about your parents, if I were you."

76

"No . . . ?"

"How many times have they written to you since you've been here?"

"Once, but they've a lot on and letter-writing's not their thing . . ."

"And neither are you by now. Face up to it: we're freaks and everyone we meet will always, sooner or later, be glad to be shot of us . . ."

Before he could say anything to this, the door opened behind him, and they both looked round, almost guiltily.

It was Peter Farley.

"I've been looking everywhere for you," he said to Martin.

"Why?"

"You're wanted."

"What for?"

"Another Games session . . ."

"You'd best get going, then," Sue said, moving her lamp closer to her work.

\*

Doll's visitor was with him again, and the two of them watched, through the two-way mirror, Martin playing the Game with Peter Farley. The visitor was tall and grey-haired . . . indeed, greyness seemed to be his prevailing colour—or lack of it. Eyes, hair, skin, even his clothes gave an impression of lifeless neutrality which only the quick movements of his head, as he looked from Farley to Martin, contradicted.

"He's had twenty minutes," the man said. His accent was strange . . . definitely not English, but difficult to identify as that of any particular foreign country.

"He can go on a bit longer yet," Doll replied, not taking his eyes off Martin.

"I hope and pray you know what you are doing," the man whispered, but Doll ignored him.

Martin's head was aching and he felt sick and dizzy. More than anything else, he wanted to be out of the close and oppressive atmosphere of that room and into clean and fresh air. But Farley's eyes held him captive; he could not escape them. When he tried to move, his limbs were leaden and beyond his control.

For the twentieth time he was being taken back to the huts and the death of the bird, and, under the fierce and endless questioning, he was becoming the bird, forever struggling to rise in flight, but always being brought down to death in the muddy earth.

"Think carefully," Farley insisted, but Martin was almost past thinking at all. "Think it through. There was nothing in that hut but scientific stores. I have told you that and you believe me." He paused, leaning even closer to the boy, across the cheap wooden table. "Don't you . . . ?"

Martin didn't reply, but sat, large-eyed, staring at him.

"Of course you do, since there is no reason for me to lie to you. Therefore, nothing can have harmed that bird. Therefore it did not die. *Therefore* . . . therefore what, Martin?"

"I don't know . . . I don't . . ." Martin whispered.

"You *do* know! *Therefore what?*"

"I must have . . ."

"Yes, go on, must have what . . . ?"

Martin was struggling now, fighting against the words that he had to say. He was bent over, hands clenched between his knees, eyes closed. "Dreamt it . . ." he gasped.

Farley's voice rose even higher, became even more penetrating. "No! You didn't! Face it and say it!"

"Imagined it," Martin uttered.

"I don't hear you! Speak louder!" Farley shouted.

"Imagined it!" Martin shouted back.

But Farley wouldn't let him be: "Why should you do such a thing?"

"I don't know . . ."

"Don't you?" Farley asked, his voice calm and friendly now as he leant back in his chair. "No. Of course you don't. Then let me tell you. In your *conscious* mind you have no knowledge of this . . . but in your *subconscious* mind the truth is there, scurrying into a dark corner, afraid."

"What is the truth?" Martin whispered, looking up at him now.

"That you are that bird, flying high, fighting the earth pull that will drag you down. So strongly do you feel this that you believe that you have seen a thing happen. To a bird. To *you*."

Martin closed his eyes again, but this time there was no tension in him. It was as if he had fallen asleep. When he spoke, his voice was so faint that Farley had to lean in to him to hear it.

"It is not true," he said.

"It *is* true. Now that you have seen inside that hut you *know* that it is true, but your hidden fears are true too. Outside Falconleigh there is the world that will destroy you, drag you down. The world is the earth pull that will use and kill you. Where, then, are you safe, Martin?"

"Nowhere safe . . ."

"Not true, Martin . . . not true. Here. *Here*. Safe. Protected. Secure. Valued. Away from the mocking jostle of the playground. Away from the fool of a teacher who didn't know and didn't want to know . . ."

Martin was still trying, but it was a losing battle. "Home . . . this isn't home . . ."

"Home for your body . . . ? Or home for your mind? And which is the better part of you, Martin?"

The room was spinning around him: at the far end of a long and circling tunnel he could only see Farley's eyes, hear distantly his voice . . .

*

79

In the control room, behind the two-way mirror, the stranger was standing, hands pressed against the glass. "Stop it!" he shouted. "Tell him to stop!"

"The mike's off and he can't hear you, but I'll tell him to stop, if that's what you want," Doll said, switching the microphone on. "That's it, Peter: go to the slides . . ."

The man was still staring at Martin through the glass. "There will be no more of this. No more! Do you understand!"

"He has to be kept here; you know that," Doll replied, his voice emotionless.

"I would rather he were chained in a dungeon than that he should suffer again what I have seen . . ." Then, as he looked at this genius child, his hands came up to his face in a gesture of horror and revulsion. "And what," he gasped, "in God's name are you doing to him now . . . ?"

For, in the middle of that vast and dark space, Martin was standing and slowly turning, as on the walls, on the ceiling, on the very floor at his feet, huge, enveloping images of a bird were flying and then, with a dreadful symmetry, falling: falling and shrieking in a death agony.

And Martin slowly bent and fell, his outstretched arms spanning the beating wings.

# SEVEN

The Falconleigh Arms had once been an outbuilding on the estate of the big house, and it shared the elegance of its parent. In season it was a favourite week-end watering-hole for discriminating city dwellers. Now, however, as the year advanced, there was only one guest in the pub, and he could be seen, leaning on the ledge of his open bedroom window, enjoying the chequered beauty of the farmlands. He was also listening, with more than ordinary interest, to Barry, as he stood in the porchway beneath his window, asking the landlord if he could pitch his tent in the orchard at the rear of the house. The landlord agreed fairly readily—at this time of the year any custom was better than none—and at that the man left his vantage point and walked back to the centre of the room. A new element had entered his strategy now, and he frowned as he placed it.

That it would have a place he had no doubt—it might even, indeed, be a bonus. He sat in an easy chair and rehearsed once more his previous plans. This was a habit with him and had been these twenty years past . . . a habit which went some way towards explaining why he was still alive when other men who had joined the Service at the same time as he were either dead or had disappeared from view somewhere in the grim cellars of the Lubianka prison. The more desperate the job, the more meticulously he would plan, and the more closely he would check those plans. He left nothing to chance. And the task before him now would call for the most precise plans he had ever laid. For the hundredth time he went through the documents on the table by his chair, but he could still find no fault in them. The office had done well. Then he sat back, slowly put himself into a state of deep relaxation and lived through his cover story. The first part was easy, for it was true: and that is the essence of a cover that can be kept. In 1967 Andy Rutherford was a grammar school boy from Leeds going up to Cambridge on an open scholarship to read physics. He had a modestly good career at University and got a decent enough second-class degree. Now fiction had to take over from fact. While the real Andy Rutherford had gone from scientific research in the Civil Service to more shadowy work in Naval Intelligence, the new man went from government employ to teaching in a minor public school—and he had a cleverly forged group school photograph at his side to prove it. From there he had gone to an Icarus Foundation school in Italy, in the Alban hills, outside Rocca di Papa. And he fervently hoped that no one would turn up from *there* during the few days that he would need at Falconleigh.

It *had* to go right. So far as he was concerned, the consequences of failure were known and accepted—they came with the job—but the wider effects of any slip up didn't bear thinking about, for they would mean that, for the first time in its long history, his country would be totally defenceless.

That was his nightmare, and it had haunted him during all the long months of work on this project: months that had begun in the most routine of ways, just before his Christmas leave.

He had known for years, of course, about our new Lancer missile—but then, who hadn't? It had been argued about, demonstrated against, postponed, re-activated, postponed again and then finally developed at a cost that swallowed up a huge chunk of the defence budget. Now it was ready for testing. There was no thought that it would do anything but fulfil the Ministry's hopes and promises, combining as it did the range and punch of anything the Yanks and the Russians had got with total control and lightning-like speed and manoeuvrability. It was superb—if you wanted a weapon that couldn't be countered and that could lay waste a hundred square miles of enemy territory. In one leap Great Britain went to the top of the league of military terror.

Andy had been given the job of heading the Naval Intelligence team sent out to observe the test firing: it was, he supposed, a sort of reward for past work well enough done. "Be a holiday for you," his boss had said. "Pacific firing range, stop over in Los Angeles . . . take a week's leave there, if you like . . ."

Thanks, Sir Hugh, he thought . . . thanks a bundle.

And, as he sat in this quiet English pub, he could see again the scene in the monitoring hut; the dancing figures of the computers and the men leaning into the light of the radar screens, and hear once more the hum of the air conditioning.

The officer in charge had grinned round at the NATO admirals, like a conjuror about to do a clever trick. "Quiet, please!" he'd said, though no one was making a sound that Andy could hear. "Damocles preparing to launch in 60sq. Firing range clear."

But Andy had only been thinking of the meal he would be ordering in—a glance at his watch—forty-three minutes time. He'd have champagne—why not, it would be a celebration—though the day's business was predictable enough not to need launching with bubbly.

From the loudspeaker by his head he'd heard the throb of

the firing submarine's engines, powerful, irresistible. One of the Admirals had turned to his neighbour. "Once the missile's fired you'll see the underwater tracking there . . ." And he'd pointed to a radar screen, a child showing off his Christmas toy.

"Damocles clear to fire. Launch in 15SQ."

Then the countdown. "Ten . . . nine . . . eight . . . seven . . . six . . . five . . . four . . . three . . . two . . . one: *zero*."

Then the sound of the tracking bleeps in the room and a sweating admiral shouting: "There she goes!"

"Tracking on red."

The bleeps again, this time more rapid.

"Tracking on green. Range 586. Coming to . . ."

But the sound of his voice trailing away as he'd lurched towards one of the screens.

The bleeps had stopped.

Silence.

The officer switching on a microphone, hand trembling and his voice, when he spoke, suddenly hoarse. "Signals vanished at eighteen-o-seven. Check satellite link. Switch to emergency system and check for jamming."

Then the phone had rung, but it was grabbed before the first observer had turned his head to it. The officer listened silently, put it down and turned to face them: "Captain Shaw on number one support vessel. Reports that Lancer blew up in mid-air."

Then there had been the secret enquiry. The reports on Andy's desk grew until they needed a filing cabinet, then two, then three. Now the room was lined with them. At the end of the day the report was unanimous: there had been no possibility of Lancer having been destroyed by a counter-weapon, or of it being sabotaged. Therefore, there must have been an electronic or mechanical malfunction. So, the

84

other missiles in the Lancer armoury were taken apart, tested, re-tested, tested yet again and then put back together again.

Andy's boss had come into his office, smelling of the after-shave that he always wore for a meeting with the Prime Minister.

"They want another firing, Andy," he'd said.

And Andy had shrugged his shoulders.

"Would you give your go-ahead?"

"Not my decision," Andy had replied. "Thank God."

"'Fraid it is, you know. You've been handling the security. They think that everything else is OK . . . but you're the judge on that one. And the PM is waiting for an answer. Go or no go?"

"It's a perfectly good missile. And no one's got at it or will get at it."

"So?"

And Andy had nodded.

The second test firing had not had the holiday atmosphere of the first. There was an intense and grim silence in the room. Andy wasn't unnoticed this time—everyone knew that the firing was taking place on his advice. From time to time one of the top brass had turned round, trying to get assurance of success from his expression; but his face gave nothing away.

The same ritual . . . the conditions ideal, the launch perfect, and the missile surging out of the water, climbing into the sky and proceeding unfalteringly to its targeting path.

It worked. Faultlessly.

The top brass were preparing the words of relief and congratulation . . . but they were too soon. As if they'd been cut off with a knife the tracking bleeps stopped. And when the phone had rung this time, the officer in charge had been in no hurry to pick it up. He knew what the message would be.

*

Andy had taken the blame, of course. He'd expected that and he wasn't grumbling. Sir Hugh had done his utmost to shelter him from the worst of it: that was the way that Naval Intelligence operated, always looking after its own, for good or ill.

Andy had questioned everyone on the firing submarine and on the support vessels, but they told him nothing that helped. Two ratings on two separate ships had thought that they'd seen a flash of bright light in the sky, well down on the very tip of the horizon at the moment when the missile had disintegrated, and that had seemed a lead worth following—it could have been evidence of a laser impulse. So Andy spent weeks interrogating defectors from the East, checking through scientific journals, interviewing again all the leading British and American scientists in the laser field, searching for the slightest clue that would indicate that the Russians had a laser gun that could have destroyed the missiles. But he always returned to the same point: their research was no nearer than ours to solving the insoluble. No laser gun was accurate enough to do such a job or light enough to be carried by a space vehicle or aircraft. And, in any event, there had been no satellite at the right firing angle, and no aircraft in the vicinity.

Lasers were out.

Then he got the shadow of a break. One of his American agents picked up a rumour of a rumour of a rumour that the US Army had knocked out a pilotless plane with a new weapon. Andy had gone straight to Sir Hugh with the news, and he'd followed it up with the Americans: but if they had information they had no intention of sharing it with him.

Blank. Big problem. But lasers, or something with the same sort of capacity, were back in again.

Supposing now, just supposing, that the Americans *and* the Russians had got their paws on to a laser gun that was light enough to be transported, that was totally accurate at long range . . . that wasn't coming out of their own research programmes. Bad thought. Someone must have sold them the know-how. Who?

Anonymous scientists? It was a contradiction in terms —any scientist who'd cracked *that* one would be on the roof-tops and crowing his head off. As a breed, their conceit made opera singers seem like novices in a convent.

All the same, *if* the big boys *had* got hold of something then they must have got it from somewhere—or from someone. An individual or a group . . . Yes, it would have to be a group, you couldn't go alone on this one . . . unbelievably brilliant and totally anonymous.

What an inconceivable combination!

The pressure on him mounted. If two missiles could be wiped from the sky as easily as a cat knocks down a bird, then all our missiles could suffer the same fate.

He worked longer and longer hours: nothing that could possibly, or even impossibly, solve the problem was overlooked. His team grew in size. The finest scientists in the Ministry of Defence were working for him, the brightest of the university people were read the Official Secrets Act and interviewed even more pressingly. Still nothing. No one had solved the laser problems.

It was as if he were searching for a ghost.

The strain began to take its toll. He was totally exhausted. One night, sitting in that silent building as darkness fell, his brain felt as if it had turned to dust in his head. Wearily, he rang the bell for his assistant. She came in to the office, looked at the mess of charts, graphs and reports that

87

littered the desk and the floor and, without speaking, began to put the papers into their boxes and cabinets. "You look all in, Commander," she said, as she slammed the last drawer shut, "and you're doing no good flogging yourself like this. None at all."

He didn't say anything, but he knew that she was right.

"Then why don't you knock off? Go home, have a nice hot bath and watch telly?"

He nodded, got up, slung his coat over his shoulder and left the office.

He did as he'd been told and had his bath: but afterwards he had no energy to make a meal or to get dressed again to go out to eat. This, he reflected, was when a wife would be good: someone to smooth his brow with one hand while slipping an omelette in front of him with the other. Permanent relationships of that kind had not, however, been his thing.

He'd have to settle for whatever was in the larder. He flicked the television set on and wandered through into the kitchen. Sardines seemed to be the only delight on offer.

He could half hear the television in the next room while he struggled with the stupid key opener: some sort of science competition for kids seemed to be on. He scraped the sardines on to a plate, smothered them with black pepper and made some coffee. Then, cup in one hand and plate in the other, he made his slow way back into the living-room. The television was showing a close-up of a grinning boy, then the camera cut to a middle-aged academic giving an award to a group of smiling schoolgirls who'd done something very clever in chemistry. He heard the phrase "young scientist of the year", then the academic bloke was holding forth about young minds having a brilliant originality often denied to more experienced . . .

Andy didn't realise that he was slowly pouring his coffee all over his living-room carpet.

*

Andy didn't sleep that night. It was a wild thought, his wildest among many, but then he'd tried everything else. Perhaps it wasn't as wild as all that—he remembered his prof. at Cambridge telling him that all decent mathematicians and physicists were burned out by the time they were twenty-five. He thought of the greats: Einstein, Froelich —they certainly seemed to fit the bill. Supposing then that someone had got hold of a child genius of that sort of stature . . . or maybe more than one . . . that would make even more sense—if those children could be directed into certain areas of work, and the results *combined* . . .

A school was what he was looking for: a school for super-bright children.

He was first in the queue outside the British Library next morning, and he asked for every reference book they had on special schools for clever children in every country in the world. He worked right through the day, and his notebook got fuller. By the time that the library closed he decided he could allow himself a lot of food and a bottle of good wine. He went to his favourite Italian restaurant.

While he ate he went through his notebook, ticking some entries, putting crosses against others. By the end of the meal he had cut his list by half, but it was still very long. He had no idea that there were so many schools of this sort, though not many of them were British. Either we don't have many bright kids, he thought, or we don't think much of the ones we've got.

By the next morning, he had not only a final list of possible schools, but he'd also listed the questions that he needed the computer to sort out for him. By five past nine the computer clerk had the papers and he was in his boss's room.

One of the many good things about working for Sir Hugh Francis was that he was never surprised or shocked by anything: if the Prime Minister had defected to the KGB he would merely have inclined his very bald head and made arrangements for a committee meeting to discuss the vetting of the successor.

So Andy wasn't surprised by the easy response that his wild idea received. "Interesting thought" was the only comment. Then Sir Hugh pressed a button on his intercom, and, almost immediately, the computer clerk came into the room, carrying the print-out of Andy's schools.

"What made you tell him to come straight to you?" Andy asked, as the clerk went out.

"You weren't in yesterday and no one knew where you were . . . then a friend of mine spotted you in the BM and happened to see your reading list. Quite straightforward really. Now," he said, reaching over for the print-out, "might I glance at this?"

"Be my guest."

He read quickly, nodding once or twice and making occasional notes in the margin of the sheet. Then he looked across at Andy, taking off his gold rimmed spectacles and slowly polishing them. "Seems to me that your list can be narrowed down to a couple of organisations: only they have the resources and the international dimension. Of those two, I would urge you to consider this one." He underlined one of the names on the paper and passed it across the desk.

"The Icarus Foundation," Andy murmured. "Peculiar sort of name for a group of schools . . ."

"Somewhat odd . . . in the myth, of course, Icarus was a high flyer, so that part connects . . . but he fell to earth, or rather to sea, with quite a splash. However, let's not worry too much about that. Have a look at them, Andy—see what you can find out. I notice that their English school is called Falconleigh. Do you know where that is?"

Andy shook his head. "Haven't a clue."

"Well, wherever—I think that I'd like you to keep away from it. No sense in stirring up trouble. Confine yourself to the general background—links between the various schools and so on—"

"You think that there might be something in it . . . as an idea?"

"That we don't know, do we . . . ? But I'm sure you'll soon find out." He put his spectacles back on and replaced his handkerchief in his top pocket, always sure signs that an interview was over. "And Andy—go carefully—I have something of a feeling that toes, if trodden on, might prove to be sensitive . . ."

Andy had asked his questions: over long lunches in expensive and exclusive clubs, over beer and nuts in Fleet Street bars, over cups of tea in suburban cafes, over copies of the *Financial Times* in commuter trains and under heavy Victorian statuary in corridors of the House of Commons.

At the end of the week he knew as much about the Icarus Foundation as anyone outside it possibly could. He knew that three very senior civil servants were on the Board of Governors of Falconleigh and that one of them was on the international committee of management. That man, and one of the others, were in the Ministry of Defence. Suspicious? No, he thought, not really—Eton and Harrow gathered such people to their governing bodies too, and he'd nothing in this connection against *them*.

But he was getting a certain feeling about the Icarus

Foundation: something intangible, but very real. The answers to some of his questions had seemed to swim away, like fish into reeds.

He was now quite sure that all was not well in those schools, and that, innocently or otherwise, some very highly placed people were deeply involved.

He went back to Sir Hugh.

"It couldn't be, could it, that *we're* customers of Icarus? Buying research information, that sort of thing?"

Sir Hugh inclined his head and considered the thought. "Andy, you don't know that *anyone* is, you've not brought me a speck of proof . . ."

"No. I haven't. But—could we be?"

"Isn't that what you're trying to find out?"

"Right."

"Then you must keep on, mustn't you?" And, very firmly, he put his spectacles on.

*

And, for the next week, keep on he did. More interviews, more nights spent analysing his information; but still no evidence that could be used, only his deepening suspicion.

He came into the office after an unusually late night and saw Sir Hugh at the end of the long ground-floor corridor. That was odd—like seeing a lion in the supermarket. Then he stopped the tea lady as she trundled her urn and took a cup. That was strange too, for he hated the stuff. Then he turned, cup in hand, and, as casually as could be, swung the axe: "I'm taking you off this project, Andy."

Just as calmly as that, with no warning.

"You can't!"

"I'm afraid I can, you know. In fact, from this moment on, you're beginning indefinite leave."

This was incredible and Andy swallowed hard. "You mean I'm suspended?"

Sir Hugh took a sip of tea and grimaced at the taste of it. "I didn't use the word."

"You didn't have to."

"I simply want you to keep away from the office for a while."

"I see. Might I ask why?"

"You weren't getting anywhere—and the powers that be are very impatient people."

"On the contrary: I *was* getting somewhere, and that's the trouble, isn't it?"

"Meaning?"

"Meaning that the Icarus Foundation has some very good friends."

Sir Hugh shook his head, regretfully, like a doctor giving bad news. "No. It isn't that. Icarus is a dead end. There's nothing there. You have to accept that."

"I don't think I have to accept anything of the kind."

"Commander: I'm giving you an order."

Andy paused for a moment before turning away. "Very good, Sir Hugh. Order received."

And he walked out, into the traffic and bright sunlight of the indifferent London street.

He went back to his flat to destroy his notes. By training and inclination he always obeyed orders, there was no room in the Service for buccaneers. But, as he looked at them, his instinct, that blind feeling, told him that he was right. None the less, he switched on the paper shredder. It was someone else's problem now, and there was nothing more that he could do about it.

Or was there? The papers in his hand were on the very edge of the meshing knives of the machine . . . but he didn't put them in. He thought of the stakes in this game—they were the highest he had ever known. Were they so high, though, that they could justify him in ignoring a direct order?

He switched the machine off, went back into the living-room and dialled a telephone number, hating what he was about to do, and knowing that the consequences of failure would be too terrible to contemplate. To disobey Sir Hugh Francis was to kiss obliteration . . .

\*

And now he sat, in his bedroom at the Falconleigh Arms, and thought of the way ahead. Whatever happened he was in great danger. If he was right, and the Icarus Foundation *was* peddling high grade scientific military information to whoever was in the market, then they weren't likely to play ring-a-ring-a-roses with anyone who blew the gaff. And if he'd got it wrong, Sir Hugh would blast his career and any other he tried to follow as completely as if he'd never been born.

And he'd committed others, too . . . Madge, in the office, who'd made his forged papers and was acting as his back up . . . Ted and Harold, his heavies, who were standing by for his instructions. If he went down on this one, they'd drown with him.

He had to be right, and it had to go right.

He put the documents and photographs in his pocket and walked over to the window. The big lad who'd arrived the night before was sitting outside his tent, wiping over his shoes with a piece of rag. Looks, Andy thought, as if he was going visiting . . . to his kid brother at the school, probably.

He quickly left the window and walked out of the room.

Barry looked up as Andy came towards him. He thought at first that the landlord must have changed his mind about letting him camp in the orchard, and that this man was coming to tell him to clear out. There was something official-looking about him—a sort of policeman type—but then his cheery grin set Barry's mind at rest.

"Bit chilly for this sort of thing," the man said.

"Not really. Anyway, I'm used to it . . . I do Outdoor Education at school."

"That's good. Mine host was telling me something about you having a brother at the school here . . ."

"Yeah . . . our Martin."

"Thought they'd have put you up there if you'd come down to see him."

Barry shook his head and looked away.

"By the way, my name's Andy Rutherford, I'm staying at the pub."

Barry got to his feet to shake hands. "Barry Smith."

"Feel like a drink? It's just on opening time."

"Thanks all the same, but I'm under eighteen, and they know it—so they won't serve me."

"I'd put you at more than eighteen. Anyway, let's see if they can give us some coffee . . ."

Gradually, over the coffee, Andy heard the whole story: Barry's doubts about Martin coming to the school in the first place, how they could never get in touch with him, and how the school discouraged visitors. Barry told Andy that he'd gone along last night, but that he'd been given the heave ho before he'd even got to the doors of the building. "All visits are strictly by appointment" they'd said, but when he'd tried to make an appointment he'd been fobbed off with some tale that Martin was in the very middle of important work and couldn't be disturbed.

"What are you going to do, then?" Andy asked.

"Try again; I don't give up easy."

By the set of this lad's jaw, Andy thought, that would most certainly be true. "All the same, if they turfed you out once, what makes you think they'll let you in now?"

"Maybe I won't ask, this time."

"Take the law into your own hands, so to speak?"

"It's our kid in there!"

"Oh, I see that! Still, whatever you do, be careful."

It was late afternoon when Barry returned. As Andy watched him walk up the road he could tell from his expression that he'd been no more successful this time than before. He walked to meet him.

"No joy?"

Barry shook his head. "I tried sneaking in through the bushes at the side there . . . a couple of gardeners headed me off before I'd gone twenty yards."

"They keep their eyes open . . ."

"Bit more than that," Barry said. "They've got telly cameras in the trees."

"You're joking!"

"True . . . they can see every blooming thing! And the gardeners have got walkie talkie sets. They're on to you quick as a flash."

"All a bit odd, for a school, isn't it?"

"That's what I thought. Place is more like a prison!"

They were outside the door of the pub now. "So what next?" Andy asked.

"I'll think of something."

"So will I."

Barry turned towards him, doubt and suspicion in his eyes. "What's it to you, then?"

"Nothing. Nothing at all. But I'm very curious . . . and this trip was becoming very boring: none of the farmers round here seem to be very interested in my firm's products. So you're putting a bit of interest into very dull days . . ."

\*

Martin was in his room, still sleeping, and the injection he'd been given would ensure that he stayed like that for another five hours, at least.

The two men stood, by the side of his bed, looking at him: Doll casually, his hands in his pockets, and the grey-haired man tensely, leaning over the bed.

"He'll be all right," Doll said. "Won't remember a thing when he comes round."

"You had better be right, my friend."

"Of course I'm right! I know what I'm doing: dammit all, he's a kid like any other kid . . . they survive worse than this."

"No!" the man cried. "He is not like any other! Have you really no idea who you are dealing with here? Not just another clever child whose mind may be picked like a safe! In him, this boy, we are face to face with Galileo, Newton, Einstein! Are you not even scientist enough to know blasphemy when you commit it?"

Doll walked away from him, towards Martin's table, and the neat pile of notes on top of it. "I know who I'm dealing with—these notes—"

"Are totally beyond your understanding!"

Doll wheeled round. "That's as maybe! But one thing's for sure . . . I know what *you'll* do with them . . ."

There was silence between them: the stranger looked at Doll, his eyes cold as ice. "So . . . amaze me," he whispered.

Doll's gaze faltered and he looked away from him. "World powers—our clients, not content with atom bombs or hydrogen bombs are panting like dogs for the ultimate weapon . . ."

"And what is that?"

"The quark bomb . . ."

"And you think that the groundwork for such a terrible thing is there—in those papers?"

"I know it. I am scientist enough for that."

"No," the man said. "It may be that this boy has taken a step: many others would be needed."

"He could take them."

"That we don't know."

"But we do know," Doll said, coming to the end of the bed, "that in the challenges you will set him, you will keep him on that path . . ."

"You see me, then, as gravedigger to the world?" the man asked, his voice quiet.

"I see you as I have always seen you."

The man smiled, but it was a wintry smile. "But you have not 'always seen me', only since I gave you employment —and I begin to think that I was mistaken in doing that." And he went towards the door. "There will be no more criminal foolishness with this boy . . . you forget that at your great peril, Mr Doll . . ."

\*

The bar at the Falconleigh Arms did a fair amount of business during the summer months, but now, as the nights were drawing in, it was almost deserted. A couple of regulars stood at one end of the bar, swapping jokes, and Andy sat behind his newspaper at a table at the opposite end. So, when the door opened and another customer came in, they all looked round, and the barmaid put on a welcoming smile. "Mr Farley!" she cried. "Long time since we've seen you!"

"Bit busy, these days. Twenty of my usual cigarettes, please, Nora."

She went to the display stand at the back of the bar, calling over her shoulder as she reached for the cigarettes, "Boy staying here reckons his brother's up at the school."

"Yes? Who'd that be, then?"

"Smith, says his brother's called Martin—least, that's what I *think* he said . . ."

"Pupil of mine, actually . . ."

"I'll get his brother, he'd love to meet you—" And she lifted the flap at the end of the bar.

"Don't bother, Nora," he said, pushing the flap down again. "I really haven't time tonight . . . I only popped in for these. Anyway, I hate meeting relatives when I'm off duty . . ."

"He'll be ever so disappointed . . ."

Andy put his newspaper down and walked over to the bar, looking closely at Farley. Then he slapped the counter, his face a picture of delighted surprise. "Well!" he cried, "As I live, move and have my being! It's Peter Farley isn't it?"

Farley turned towards him. "I'm sorry," he said, "I don't think I . . ."

"Cambridge!" Andy shouted, giving him a playful punch in the ribs. "I was at Downing . . . you were at King's!" Farley still didn't seem to recognise him and stood, looking very blank, but Andy wasn't being put off. "I *am* right . . . aren't I? You are the selfsame chap?"

"I am Peter Farley—and I was certainly at King's. But I can't seem to . . ."

"Rutherford, Andy Rutherford, it'll come back to you in a minute. What brings you to this neck of the woods, then? Hold on—while you're thinking, I'll get some drinks in." He was already signalling to the barmaid, holding lightly on to Farley's arm the while. "Two pints of best bitter, please love!" Then he turned back to Farley, as happy as if he'd just bumped into his best friend in the middle of the Gobi desert. "You were about to tell me what you were doing down here . . ."

"Schoolmastering."

"What, with a degree like yours! I don't believe it! I'd have put you down for something tremendous! Top class scientific research . . . something like that." Nora brought their drinks across and Andy steered Farley into a seat. "Good school, is it? Where you're teaching?"

99

"Very—anyway, it suits me . . ."

"Well . . . so long as you're happy, I say. Cheers!"

*

When Martin woke up, he was sitting, fully dressed, in the chair by his desk. The bed that had been brought into his room had been taken away again: not that he had any memory of being in it, or of anything since he'd started on the calculation that lay, unfinished, before him. He felt very hungry and looked at his watch, then realised that he must have missed supper—but he had done that too often in the past for it to be remarkable. He walked over to the communication panel, flicking the switch that would put him through to the kitchens. "Big plate of egg and chips, please," he requested.

"Certainly, sir. Ten minutes: is that all right?"

"Fine . . . and lots of bread and butter and a pot of strong tea!"

"Very good, sir."

He went back to his work, feeling happier than he'd been in a long time.

When the food arrived, he had almost forgotten that he'd ordered it, his work was so engrossing. He pointed to the edge of his table and the waiter silently put the plates there, poured him a cup of tea and left him to it: "do not disturb" should have been the school motto.

Martin forked the food into his mouth with his left hand and carried on working with his right; when he found that the plate was empty he put it on the floor, and it was as he was straightening up from this that Sue came in.

"Where've you been, then?" she asked.

"Working."

"Oh. I came by once or twice, but your door was locked."

"Didn't want to be interrupted."

That was explanation enough for both of them—they

were, after all, describing normality at Falconleigh.

"There's a disco on tonight. You coming?"

"I dunno," he replied. "I've a lot on."

"Do you good . . . just look at you, white as a sheet! You can do too much work, you know, even for this place."

He looked at his papers: he was nearly finished anyway. "Might as well," he said. "What time?"

"About an hour?"

"See you then."

\*

An Englishman of Farley's background can resist most things; threats and violence most easily, but courtesy defeats him completely. So it was that he now sat behind a row of empty beer glasses two hours after he had meant to leave the pub. Every time that he got up to go, another pair of full glasses appeared and he wearily sat down again. Once he'd almost made his escape, when this awful Rutherford bore went off to go to the loo or make a phone call or something, but he'd been back again before he'd got through the doorway, two more foaming glasses in his hands, gently nudging him back to his seat.

Not that the drink had loosened Farley's tongue; if that had been Andy's plan it had failed completely. Farley felt a little bit sick, but he was as clear-headed and discreet as ever.

Now, however, their glasses were empty again, and he seized his chance, standing up and saying, very firmly: "I really *have* to go."

Andy looked at his watch. "Good Lord! I didn't know it was that time! You've been keeping me from my bed, old friend—promised myself an early night."

Farley grinned, weakly. "Might say the same for you . . ."

"I'll see you to your car."

"No need to bother," Farley said, afraid that passing the

bar on the way out might set off another bout of ale swigging.

"No bother, I could do with a breath of air."

And, wonder of wonders, they got outside and into the car park.

"Which is yours?"

"That one," Farley said, pointing to a newish BMW.

"Nice job," Andy exclaimed, walking up to it and slapping the bonnet. Then he bent down, peering at the trim below the door. "I say, though—don't want to worry you, but you've got a bit of rust starting there . . ."

"Where?" Farley asked, wondering as he bent down how he'd managed to see it in the dark.

"Just there," Andy replied as he brought his fist down in an exceptionally neat rabbit punch on the back of Farley's neck.

That was the last that Peter Farley knew of the evening.

Two large men moved very quickly out of the shadows. One took Farley's driving keys from his limp hand and leapt into the car, while the other dragged the unconscious body to the back of a small van and, helped by Andy, bundled it inside. Within three minutes they were both away, leaving Andy alone in the car park. "Thanks Ted, thanks Harold," he murmured as he turned to go back into the pub.

It had gone very nicely, he thought, with not a soul to notice it.

But he was wrong there. Barry had been getting into his tent . . . and he hadn't missed a thing.

# EIGHT

Falconleigh discos were good: superb equipment and the latest records. There was a notebook in Recreation One; the kids wrote down what they wanted and it was there within a couple of days.

Sue and Martin could hear the sound of the music as they walked up the path, but when they opened the doors the full blast of it hit and held them, and they stood in the doorway, letting it take them. Their eyes were dazzled by the brilliance of the images that covered them and the whole room, making another world out of that space: a disturbing world, holding a threat of violence, pulsating with the raw beat of the music. And those abstract dangerous images, cast on to faces, on to walls, on to the ceiling, stirred memories in Martin's mind and unlocked an imprisoned thought. His body went tense and he started to sweat, then he relaxed. He was free of something, although he didn't know what.

"Are we dancing, then?" Sue shouted.

"In a minute," he replied. Somewhere in this room there was both a question and an answer, and he had to find them. He looked across the dancers to the girl who was working the equipment and acting as DJ. He'd spoken to her once or twice—she was a physicist too, though working in a different area from him. Her name was Frances, he remembered, Frances Greene—something like that. "Won't be long," he shouted to Sue, and pushed his way through the couples on the floor towards Frances.

"Quite a set-up," he said, when he got to her, his voice high over the music.

"Not bad," she yelled back. "Need to build a few more things in, though."

"You mean you made it yourself?"

"Yeah. Watch this!" She flicked a switch, adjusted the controls and a group of fantastic dancers arose out of nowhere and leapt towards them.

"Very clever," he nodded. "Lasers?"

"Laser holography."

"Brilliant!"

"This is just for giggles . . . the real work's something else again."

"Where do you do that, then?"

"One of the huts back of the house."

The question was known now, and answered. A deep, fierce anger gripped his gut and he had to look away for a moment to cover it. But hiding his feelings came easily to Martin: he'd had practice, and his voice was loud but level when he spoke again.

"Love to see it."

She shook her head. "Not on."

"No?"

"Boss's orders. It's kept locked up—always. Matter of fact, I shouldn't have mentioned it even to you. Jacko says that I've got to keep it under wraps."

"Why?"

"Well, it's not all my own work, you see, most of the theory was worked out by kids in other Icarus schools. We really just put it all together here: he says it's not fair on them if I go blurting it out."

"Don't worry," he said. "I won't tell him."

"You sure?"

"'Course. This hut—I bet you've got a key."

"Right."

"Could I borrow it? You've told me so much that it wouldn't make much odds if I had a look, just for five minutes."

"No way," she said, and he could see that she meant it.

Sue came up to them—she wasn't pleased. "We came here to dance," she said, sharply.

Martin gave her a tight-lipped grin and shrugged his shoulders. "If that's your thing . . ."

"It's supposed to be everybody's thing at a disco."

"I wondered about that," he shouted, as they joined the dancers.

"What was all that about?"

"Me meeting a very interesting girl. Do you mind?"

"Why should I?"

Then the interesting girl herself danced up to them and slipped a key into his trouser pocket. "Five minutes," she whispered.

"This is turning into a beautiful evening," Sue snapped.

"It'll get better," he said, as he grabbed her wrist and pulled her off the dance floor. "We're going for a walk . . ."

\*

Doll and his visitor stood at the top of the entrance steps. The man was carefully wrapping a scarf round his neck against the chill of the evening. From the other side of the copse that bordered the drive they could hear the helicopter engine warming up.

"What time will you get there?" Doll enquired.

"Not more than an hour, it's a short flight. I shall be there by eleven."

"That's good. Well, safe journey." He walked back into the doorway, but as he did so, his attention was taken by a glimmer of light among the trees—it was a light that shouldn't be there.

"Someone's in the laser room," he said.

The man turned to him from the foot of the steps. "Laser room? That work is finished and the equipment dismantled. I gave you clear instructions . . ."

"Which have been carried out . . . the room's empty."

"I hope, Mr Doll, that you are telling me the truth —to maintain a project after completion is the most dangerous . . ."

"I've told you," Doll interrupted. "The hut's empty."

"Good. And the boy Smith—no more nonsense with him. All right?"

Would he never leave, Doll wondered; or was he to stand here being hectored and badgered for ever. "We'll look after him," he replied.

"See that you do." He looked up at Doll, outlined against the light of the hall, and he felt again his dislike and mistrust of the man. That appointment had been a mistake and it would have to be corrected. The sands of Doll's time at Falconleigh were running out fast; it might have to be that his life would run out with them. But that was a decision for the full committee, thank God. "My case," he said, "carry it to the helicopter, would you?"

Doll hesitated for a moment before coming down the steps: he wasn't anybody's servant, and time that should be spent investigating the light in the laser hut was being wasted. But when the old man was in this mood it was as well to do what he wanted. He picked up the bulging brief-case and they walked in silence together towards the landing pad.

\*

Martin and Sue stood in the hut, looking round at the banks of controls and dials and at the large lamp-like object in the centre of the floor. He left her and walked towards a console, quickly assessing the functions of the switches. He selected one and pressed it. "This is a clever trick. Watch!" A panel in the roof slid back: they could hear the helicopter engine and the pulse of the disco.

"What's that for?" she said.

"Don't you know? Don't you know what all this stuff's for?"

The blazing anger in his voice frightened her. She shook her head.

"Lasers."

"So . . . what's wrong with that?"

"What's wrong?" he shouted. "What's *wrong*? Are you an idiot? What's wrong is that they're here to kill, that's all . . . or maybe that's all right with you. *Is it*?"

"No! No, it's not all right, it's not!"

There was an empty cardboard box at his feet and he savagely kicked it into a corner of the room. "Falconleigh!" He spat the word out.

"Falconleigh's more than this room! This is just one student who . . ."

He didn't give her a chance to finish. "A bird . . . free, beautiful, in its place . . . was killed by that thing . . ." He stretched an arm towards the lamp. "Not by direct hit —that would have burned it to a second of blinding white dust—but because it dared to come near it, and that was enough. They deal in death at this place, and I want no more of it."

"It's not true . . . it can't be!" she whispered.

"Oh, yes, but it is!" He came near to her, holding her shoulders tightly. "Your work here, those famous 'challenges' that they set. What's it to do with?"

She shook her head, struggling to get away from him. "Leave go! You're hurting me!"

"*What's it to do with?*" he shouted.

"You're not a biologist, you wouldn't understand!"

"Keep it simple and try me—and be quick: we haven't much time . . ."

"Heredity." He let her go and sat down on a lab stool; but his eyes still held her, black and intense against the whiteness of his face. "Passing on of certain features from parents to offspring—like long ears and a certain colour of fur in rabbits . . ." He didn't speak or move: his body was bent towards her, tense and straining. "That's the sort of thing . . ." she said, her voice trailing into silence.

"That's already been worked out."

"No. We're only at the beginning of it."

He turned away from her, putting his head in his hands, elbows on knees in an arch of concentration. "The practical part of it?" he asked.

"You breed a better rabbit."

Very slowly, he turned back to her. "People?" he asked, his voice so low that she didn't hear him.

"What?"

"Could you make a man? Make him as you wanted him to be? A man who'd do what he was told and never question it?"

She frowned. "Cloning? Theoretically, it's possible . . . but practically I'd think that I was miles away from that."

"Maybe you are: but just maybe there's another kid in another school who's been given another bit of the sort of work you're doing, then yet another kid who—"

"Stop it!" she shouted, covering her ears. "Falconleigh isn't like that! It isn't! It isn't!"

He pulled her hands down and held her close, so close that the warmth of his breath was on her face. "Let me tell you about *my* work—and I hope to God that you can bear the weight of it—"

"I want to go back: please, Martin!"

"In a minute. I'm into sub-atomic physics. Nothing wrong with that. Nothing. But the 'challenges' I've been set are leading to something—something so dreadful—" He was swaying slightly, with his eyes tight shut.

"Falconleigh's given me everything! Don't take it away from me. Please. Please!"

"Take it away?" he said, his voice expressionless. "Take away your cosy room and anything you want when you want it? I'm telling you, if my sums come out right, everything will be taken away from everyone." He paused. "A bomb. A very special bomb, that will make anything they've got now seem like a squib you set off on Guy Fawkes' night."

"And you're near it?"

"Pushing at the door . . . and when that door opens it opens on a sight of the world as a poisoned cinder in silent space . . ."

*

The music in the disco was louder than ever and the images of the light show more savage, threatening. The room was hot and frantic with movement—when the kids at Falconleigh let themselves go, there were no bounds set.

The door opened, a cold breath of air blew into the room, but no one turned towards it. Doll stood, looking round, but it was difficult for him to make out faces, all were changed and distorted by the colours and shapes that flashed across them. Then he saw Martin, dancing, caught for a moment in white light. Their eyes met and Doll knew, by the boy's tense and bitter smile, who it was who had been in the laser room.

There were questions to be answered now, and Martin's life would be in the balance with the answers.

Someone put a drink into Doll's hand; still watching Martin he raised the glass to his mouth and drank.

*

Andy and Barry had the dining-room to themselves. The morning sunlight fell on the white tablecloth and lanced off the coffee-pot.

"I could have told the fuzz," Barry said, keeping his voice low.

"Yes. You could. So . . . why didn't you?"

"I don't know," Barry frowned. "Maybe I felt that you were on my side—and our Martin's—and this was part of it."

"Let me pour you another coffee," Andy said. He looked at Barry and noticed that his hands were trembling slightly. He wondered how much he could tell this lad, how far he could be trusted. "Your brother, Martin. I think he's in danger in that place."

Barry put his cup down. "What sort of danger?"

"Not just him—all the children . . ."

"And that's why you bashed that fellow?"

It was no use—he'd have to trust him. "Barry . . . what I'm going to tell you now is for you only. If you tell anyone else, then your brother's in real trouble. Do you understand that?"

Barry nodded, and Andy told him all that was safe to tell.

At the end of it Barry was silent, playing about with a coffee spoon in the sugar. When he finally spoke, he didn't look at Andy; it was as if he was apologising for the fancifulness of what he was saying. "Brothers can have . . . feelings, you know, something you can't explain. And right from the first I knew that place was wrong. We share something more than a name you know. . . ."

Andy nodded.

"So . . . what are we going to do?" Barry said.

"I'm going in there. Now, first thing *you've* got to do is ring your parents, tell them you'll be staying here for another few days, that you've seen Martin and that he's all right. We don't want them coming down on us at this particular moment. Then stand by and wait for instructions: there'll be something for you to do—I don't know what yet—but I promise you, you'll be very necessary before we get to the finish of this one . . ."

\*

The man who was closest to John Doll was seldom seen by the children or the staff, but, together with his assistants, he was the one who saw most of them. For hours at a time this man sat in his control room, his eyes flicking from one television monitor to another. Every room in the house had its hidden camera, and every action was noted by him and, if he thought it necessary, recorded so that Doll could see it too. It was a good system.

He was in Doll's office now, leaning over the desk.

"Peter Farley?" Doll cried. "This is absolutely ridiculous!"

"He's gone, all the same."

"But where can he have gone? Where?"

"He's nowhere in the house or grounds, that's for sure. Nor has he been since he went to the village for a packet of fags, last night."

Before they could get any nearer to a solution of this problem, there was a knock at the door. Doll nodded to the controller, who slipped out quietly through a door at the other side of the office.

"Come in!" Doll shouted.

Martin stood in the doorway. Doll had known that this meeting would have to happen sometime during the day, but he wished that he had been able to fix the time and place of it, rather than having it thrust upon him like this. None of these thoughts did he show, but put on his most welcoming smile and gestured invitingly to one of the easy chairs by the fire. "Come in, Martin, and sit yourself down."

The boy came into the room, but he didn't sit down.

"So . . . what's with you?" Doll said.

"I want out."

Doll got up from his desk and came to Martin's side. "*What* did you say?"

"Leave here."

Doll didn't immediately follow this up, but went over to the fireplace, took a pipe from the rack on the mantelshelf, slowly filled it and lit it. He didn't particularly enjoy pipe smoking, but felt that it gave him a solid, reliable image. Then he turned to Martin and slowly blew a stream of smoke towards the ceiling. "We seem to have had this conversation before. So far as I'm concerned, nothing's changed. So what's happened to you?"

"I don't have to give reasons."

"No. You don't, but this has come upon you rather suddenly, hasn't it?"

"Maybe."

"*I'd* have thought it had; and I'd have thought that a step like this would have needed an awful lot of careful consideration. Wouldn't you?"

Martin leant against the edge of the desk: his face had been pale when he came in, but it was ashen now. Doll saw that one of his knees was trembling. "You all right?" he asked.

"I know what's going on," Martin said, his voice hoarse and strained.

Doll expressed no surprise. "Oh? So what *is* going on?"

"We're being used."

Doll frowned, as if he were trying to solve a very difficult problem. "Used? For what?"

"The work we're doing."

"Is work you wanted to do. So? What about it?"

Martin didn't reply and there was silence between them. Doll turned back to the fire and noisily knocked the ash out of his pipe. "Come on, then," he said—as if he'd got other things that he ought to be doing.

"I'm working on sub-atomic particles."

"*Are* you now? Of course I leave that sort of detail to your tutor."

"You know all right—and you know what could be done with that work."

"No. I don't." He moved closer to Martin. "Tell me."

"If it came out . . . if I finished it . . . you'd have the theoretical groundwork for making a bomb . . . the most powerful ever."

Doll's expression showed his appalled surprise: "Is that true?"

"You know it."

He went back to his desk and sat, deep in thought, before he spoke. "I didn't, Martin, and that's the truth of it. But there's a couple of things I'd like you to think about. One: *any* leap forward in science can be used for good or for bad. You find a way of making very tough steel and you've given the world a smashing carving knife—or an armour piercing shell. There's a choice, but it's someone else's, not yours. Not mine. Two: my job—Falconleigh's—is to give *you* space and time for thought. Pure thought. That's all. And when the thinking's finished, it's finished."

Martin still had his back to him. "And there's the hut," he said.

"Peter Farley told me that you had some sort of obsession with that place. Look at me, Martin, please, when I'm speaking to you." Martin slowly turned to face him. "Did you break into that hut last night?"

"No. I didn't break in anywhere."

Doll slowly nodded. "Let me tell you about Frances Greene—she's quite brilliant, of course—but then everyone here is. She's been working on lasers. I backed her: the work was good. Then it went wrong, badly wrong. I stopped it. And that's the truth about the hut."

"I'm still going."

"That's entirely up to you. But have a thought as to what you'll be going back to: that nonsense of a school with its clown of a maths master . . . the ruin of all your bright promise."

"Leastways when I do my maths homework there, no one's going to die of it . . ."

"Nor here."

"Another thing: I'm not the only one who wants out."

For a moment, Doll was rattled—Martin saw the flash of shock in his eyes. "Oh? Who else?" he said, keeping his voice calm.

"Sue Kleiner."

"Then we'd better send for her too, hadn't we?" He spoke into his desk intercom. "Ask Miss Kleiner to come to see me, would you . . . she'll be in her room, I should think." Martin was still sitting on the edge of the desk. As Doll looked at him he found it difficult to conceal his dislike—if only it hadn't been this awkward unmoving lump who'd been given a genius mind! How easy it would have been with anyone else! "Might as well sit comfy while we're waiting, Martin," he said. "You look as if you're all in."

Without looking at him. Martin slid off the desk and walked towards an easy chair. Before he reached it, however, the phone rang. Martin stopped, turned towards Doll, who pulled a face to show his annoyance at this interruption and picked the phone up. He listened for a moment, then covered the mouthpiece. "Sorry about this, Martin: 'fraid it's rather a private call . . . would you mind?"

Martin nodded and walked to the door. "I'll be outside," he said.

"Right." Doll shouted into the phone, the line from Head Office was frequently bad, but today it sounded as if the woman was calling from outer space: "What's all this about? I don't understand . . ."

"Mr Farley has been recalled," the woman repeated.

"Peter Farley?"

"Surely you knew—had notice?"

"I can assure you that this is the first I've heard of it."

"There's obviously been the most ghastly slip up . . ."

"Obviously."

"We're sending you a replacement teacher."

It was too much, and his temper snapped. "I don't accept that one of my staff can be recalled between here and Falconleigh village. He hasn't packed! His stuff's still in his room!"

"A matter of loyalty," she said.

"What's that supposed to mean?"

"You know perfectly well that we can't discuss that over the telephone. Enough that he has been found to be grossly disloyal to the Foundation. There were urgent grounds for his immediate dismissal."

Doll knew, only too well, what "dismissal" from the Foundation meant. All the same, he should have been warned—unless, of course, he was under suspicion too. In that case, the replacement for Farley would be a spy, reporting back on everything he saw. He thought of the boss's recent visit, of his coolness towards him, and began to worry. "I'd like to speak to the Director of Co-ordinations, please."

"I'm afraid that's not possible. He's at Heathrow, on his

way to Innsbruck. If he should get in touch with us, we'll get him to contact you."

"Yes, do that," Doll shouted, but the woman had already put the phone down. He sat quite still, thinking about the nature of Farley's "disloyalty". He'd been Smith's tutor, so he'd have known the implications of the boy's work. . . He remembered then that Martin was still waiting outside. "Right, Martin, in you come!" he called.

"No sign of Sue?" Doll said, as the boy came in.

"No."

"She's probably into some knotty biological problem . . ." But, at that moment, there was a knock at the door and she came in.

"They said that you wanted to see me."

"That's right. Now, I don't know how best to put this, Sue—but Martin here says that you've something to tell me."

"Oh?" She wasn't looking at Martin.

"Well then . . . ?"

She shook her head. "No. Nothing to tell you."

"You sure?"

"Yes."

"Sue! You said!" Martin cried.

She turned towards him, but her eyes were on the ground. "I'm sorry, but I've changed my mind."

"That's all right, Sue," Doll murmured. "We've all got a right to do that."

"May I go now, please?" Her voice was low, frightened, like a little girl who'd been told off by a teacher.

"In a minute, Sue." He walked round to her side of the desk and sat on the edge of it, facing her. "You *were* in that hut last night, weren't you?"

"Yes."

"With him?"

"Yes!" The word was like a cry for help.

"Then . . ." But she was out of the room and running before he could say any more. He turned towards Martin. "Well . . . ?"

"You asked me if I broke in. I said I hadn't."

Doll nodded in understanding. "Frances gave you the key?"

Martin didn't answer, but moved towards the door. "Time I was off," he said.

"All packed up?"

"Yes."

"Right, then. There's a bus leaves the village in half an hour. That'll get you to the train in plenty of time. Have you any money?"

Martin shook his head.

"So what were you thinking of doing?"

"Hitching."

"And what do you suppose your parents would think of me if I let you do that? Honestly, for a bright kid, you are thick at times. Have you let them know, by the way?"

"Every time I try to get through the switchboard girl here says they must be out—there's never any reply."

"I'll get in touch with them." He opened a drawer of his desk and took a couple of ten pound notes out of a box, and held them towards Martin. "Here . . ."

"No thanks."

He walked over to him and rammed the notes into his pocket. "Just a loan."

"Thanks."

And he sounded as if he meant it, Doll thought. "I'm sorry that Falconleigh didn't work out for you."

"Yeah."

"See you . . ."

"See you," Martin replied, as he walked out of the room.

His bag was where he'd left it, by the grandfather clock in the hall. He picked it up and opened the doors on to the outside world. In front of him the drive gleamed white against the brilliant green of the grass. It dipped out of sight behind a slight rise, then appeared again, turning towards the tall trees that marked the edge of the estate. A slight cold wind was moving the tops of the trees and circling dead leaves round his feet. Then it died down and he walked in stillness, the only sound that of the gravel crunching under his feet. He thought of Sue as he walked, and wondered who in the world he could ever trust. Perhaps his mam and dad, maybe Barry—but they'd never bothered since he came here. . . .

His arm began to ache from the weight of his bag, and he stopped to change it to his other arm. He was already slightly out of breath and, though it was a cold day, he was sweating. He blinked his eyes clear and looked towards the distant trees and, although he could feel no wind now, he saw that the tops were still moving . . . swaying and dipping.

He walked on, feeling more and more weary; each step was an effort. He stopped for a rest, putting his bag down. His breathing now was forced and deep, as though he'd been running in a long race—but he had to go on, had to get through those gates. He left his bag where it was and struggled on.

The trees were moving violently now, as if they were being battered by a gale, away from him, then towards him, straining to pull free of the ground and hurtle themselves at him. All colour had gone from the blinding white sky and the trees were black against it. He looked away from them and down at his feet as they slowly dragged over the gravel. One step, then the next, the only sound his own breathing and the thumping of his heart.

\*

Andy took his foot off the accelerator as he came to the gates and swung his car into the driveway. He didn't see the boy at first: he was hidden by a dip in the ground, but then he came into view, white-faced and staggering. Instinctively Andy slammed on the brakes and the car slithered to a stop in a spurt of flying gravel. He leapt out of the car and ran, but at the sight of him the boy stopped, his face twisted into a scream, although no sound came, then turned and ran for his life back towards the school. Andy ran after him, and occasionally the boy would look over his shoulder, stumble and nearly fall. Andy could hear his sobs—in the whole of his dangerous life he had never seen anyone so frightened.

Three men came out of the doors of the school: he would have expected them to move towards the running boy, but they stood where they were, waiting. With a final effort the boy scrambled up the steps and, nearly at the top, collapsed at the men's feet.

Andy stood, trying to get his breath back. One of the men turned to the others and said: "Get him to sick bay, will you . . . they are expecting him . . ."

"Looks to be in a bad way, that lad," Andy shouted.

"Yes, he is," the man who seemed to be in charge called back. "He'll be all right now though, we'll look after him . . ."

"Good. He needs it."

"These are private grounds . . . I'd be grateful if you'd leave now," the man shouted.

"I know that, but I'm a new teacher here. My name's Rutherford. Could you tell me where I can find Mr Doll?"

Doll had come down the steps while he was speaking and the two men were now face to face. "I'm John Doll," he said.

"Have they told you I was coming?"

"Yes; but they didn't say when."

"Typical!"

"You'd better come in."

Not much of a welcome, Andy thought, but about what you'd expect under the circumstances. "I'll get my car . . . all right if I park it here?"

"Over at the side there, that's staff parking."

"And I'll pick that lad's bag up at the same time . . ."

Doll was going back up the steps, and he called over his shoulder: "See you in my office . . . first on the right after the hall."

Andy thought about the boy as he walked towards his bag, and he wondered what sorts of drugs and hypnosis they'd used to get him into that state. He fervently hoped that whoever was in charge had enough knowledge to realise that there are limits beyond which one must not go: a mistake there destroyed a mind for ever—and there could be no cure for that damage.

He opened his car door and put the bag on the floor, quickly unzipping it. Pair of binoculars, various items of clothing, then, at the bottom of the bag, a pile of papers, each one covered in formulae and calculations. It only took a glance at them to tell him that, as a scientist, he was way out of his league with this lad. He bundled the papers into the glove compartment and locked it. As he was about to zip up the bag again, he noticed a name tag on a shirt. "Martin Smith" he read, and silently thanked God that Barry hadn't seen what he had—he'd have torn those men apart.

Doll was on the phone when Andy came into his office. He nodded towards him and went on with his conversation. "Yes . . . he's here now. Do you want a word?" After a moment, he held the phone towards Andy. "It's the Director of Co-ordinations—he's at Heathrow, and it's a bad line, so you'll have to speak up."

Andy took the phone, it was indeed a bad line—all he could hear was crackle and the sounds of an airport terminal. "Hello! Mr Cantorwicz!" he bawled.

"Speaking—" a muffled voice replied.

"I'd just like to register once more my protest at being transferred like this. What's supposed to happen to the work I was doing in Italy?"

There was a mumble that could have meant anything at the other end of the line. "I shall be writing an official letter of complaint about this, I can promise you . . ." There was another squawk or two, then the line went dead. "Blighter rang off!" Andy said, as he put the phone down.

Doll nodded in sympathy. "When did you get notice that you were coming here?"

"Last night—they gave me half an hour to throw some things into a bag, then I was on the plane. It really is a bit much!"

"Quite. Have you got your papers?"

"I think so . . ." He dug into his inside pocket, got the documents out and threw them on to the desk. "Here you go . . ."

"Thanks. I'll look at them later." And he slipped them into a desk drawer.

"Nice place you've got here," Andy said as he looked out of the window.

"Yes. It's very pleasant. What were you working on in Italy?"

"Lasers. We had a very bright lad. Of course, as you know, we got a long way with the project; right to home base, in fact."

"Did you now?"

"I'd have thought that you'd have . . ."

"No. At this level we don't discuss what's going on in other schools. Surely you know that?"

"Well, of course—but in Italy it was a rule more honoured in the breach than in the observance."

"It's honoured here, all right: so try to remember that."

"Point taken," Andy grinned, but Doll didn't smile back. "I suppose I'll be doing the same sort of work here?"

"No. I don't think so."

"What then?"

"Presumably you'll take over from Peter Farley—he was tutoring the lad you met in the drive."

"The breakdown kid?"

"Yes."

"I don't much relish the thought of that, I must say. What's his thing . . . when he's well enough to do it?"

"Sub-atomic physics."

"I see."

"The important thing about Smith is that he has to be kept with us. At all costs. Is that understood?"

"Does he want to go?"

"He has certain—fantasies."

*

Martin was lying in a white-painted room next to sick bay. He was perfectly still: only his eyes moving as they followed the pictures that were being projected from behind the end of his bed on to the ceiling. And there, against a summer blue sky, a seagull silently flew.

Under his pillow there was a small tape recorder, and the murmuring voice was always in his ears.

"On the beach, Martin. On the beach. Soft, warm sand beneath you . . . feel it, let it trickle through your fingers . . ." And Martin, as he lay, lifted his hands. "You are safe, Martin . . . protected, sheltered, at Falconleigh. At Falconleigh. Only there. Safe . . ."

# NINE

Martin had never, in all his life, had the passion for work that possessed him now—every minute spent away from his papers or the computer seemed like time stolen. Food was a succession of plates of sandwiches and cups of coffee, and these, more often than not were left untouched on the tray. It was a fever that raged in him, and his eyes burned bright with the fire of it. The work was going well, and if he could just push harder, work longer, cut out the interruptions, he would finish it. Completely.

When Sue came into his room and saw him, she was appalled by his appearance. He had never been fat, but he looked emaciated now.

"Yes?" he said, impatience harsh in his voice. "You wanted something?"

"Came to see how you were."

"Well, I'm all right, aren't I . . ."

"I was worried . . . I kept asking, since the weekend."

He frowned, as if he was trying to remember something.

"While you were ill . . ."

"It was a cold, bad cold. They tell me I flaked out with it."

"I'm glad you decided to stay, anyway . . ."

"Of course I'm staying." He turned back to his table and picked up his pencil. "Look—I've a fair bit on at the minute—I'll see you later. All right?"

"I'm sorry, it's just that . . ."

"What?"

"When you wanted to go, I'd have gone with you, honest! But where could I go? Who wants me? I've nowhere but here!"

He turned towards her, but there was no sympathy in his face. "If you've got problems, see your tutor. That's what they're there for." And he went back to his work.

"Thanks," she said. "I'll do that." And she walked quickly out of the room, leaving the door open, and almost bumping into Andy in the corridor.

He watched her running away, and wondered what all that was about . . . and if it could be of any use to him. Then he went into Martin's room.

His reception wasn't exactly friendly; the boy threw his pencil into the corner of the room. "This is ridiculous!" he shouted.

"No," Andy said, smiling. "I'm your new tutor."

"What's happened to the other one?"

This kid's going to belt me in a minute, Andy thought. "Don't ask me, friend . . . got cheesed off with your untidy ways with pencils, I should think. How are you feeling, anyway?"

"Interrupted."

"This is the first day they've let me come to see you, and I won't stay long, I promise. By the way, my name's Andy Rutherford."

"Oh, yeah?"

"And you're Martin Smith, who's some sort of genius at maths." There was still that look of intense hostility from the boy. Very carefully, keeping perfectly relaxed, Andy walked over to him and looked at the papers on the desk. "Do you mind?"

"Does it matter?"

"Not much," Andy murmured as he looked through the notes. "Miles above my level, of course—but if we're to have any chance of working together, I'd better have a look see." He picked the papers up. "Is that all right?"

"You're supposed to call me 'sir'."

"So I am. Sir. Now, what else am I supposed to say? Oh, yes: is there anything I can get you . . . sir? Like the genie of the flaming lamp, I am."

"No."

"You're sure it's OK . . . my taking these?"

"Leave the top sheet."

Andy put it on the table. "Well . . . mustn't hold up genius any longer. I'll be on my way."

"One thing . . ." Martin called after him.

"Yes?"

"Could you get me a new tape for my cassette?"

"Anyone in particular?"

"Heavy rock group—use your own judgement, if you've got any."

Andy noticed the small lens of a closed circuit camera in the light fitting. "Seen that?" he asked, nodding towards it.

"Course I have—first day I was here! It's in case of fire."

"That's good. I'm a great believer in safety. Anyway, I'll get you a tape that'll blow your brains out of your ears. OK? See you then . . . sir."

Cameras in the trees, cameras in the rooms—they don't leave much to chance, Andy thought as he walked back to his room. There must be a control centre somewhere: and that would probably be worth having a look at. First things first though: the papers that he held in his hand would have to be photographed and the film sent up to one of his friends in London for analysis.

As soon as it was dark Andy made his way to the meeting point with Harold, crawling carefully through the tree camera's blind spot. He handed the package over. "It'll be there before eleven," Harold promised.

"Great stuff. How's Barry?"

"Better now he's in the pub and out of that freezing tent . . . but I don't know how long we can hold him: he's itching to have a go at someone . . ."

"I thought he might be. And Farley?"

"Complaining. Non-stop. It may be a safe house to you and me, but it's the nick to him and he doesn't like it."

When Andy got back to the school, he glanced at his watch, saw that it was supper time and strode briskly along the corridor. He had a fair bit to do, but at least now he had the chance of doing it privately.

He got the first job out of the way with little difficulty then went to Doll's office. As he expected, there was no reply to his knock. He tried the door handle, it was locked. A quick glance at it showed that it was no obstacle—it was old, beautiful and useless, and a sliver of metal that he held in his hand had it open in seconds.

Once in the room, he slipped on a pair of cotton gloves and looked round. There was a strip of light showing under the door in the opposite wall and he tip-toed over to it. Putting his ear against the panel he could hear the faint hum of electronic equipment. He smiled happily: the control room was where he'd guessed it would be. First of all, though, he needed to take a quick look round the room he was in. He tried the desk drawers; surprisingly, they were unlocked . . . but they held nothing that you wouldn't expect to find. A walk round the room told him there was no other place where anything incriminating could be stashed away. It was much as he would have expected. He took the gloves off, opened the door again and crossed to the other door in the room. He knocked on the panel.

He'd seen the man who opened the door several times round the school—he'd thought that he was a groundsman or a gardener.

"This the control room?" Andy asked.

"You've no right to be here, you know that, don't you?"

"I'm still a new boy, so I'm afraid I didn't."

"What do you want, then?"

"It's Mr Doll I was after, actually. I came into his room—the door was open, you see—then I saw the light under your door . . ."

"So?"

"I'm trying to report a fault . . . in the telephone system. The lines seem to have gone dead, and I didn't know where the switchboard was. Have you any idea where Mr Doll could be?"

"Supper."

Andy looked at his watch. "Good Lord! Is that the time! How it does fly by when you're working, doesn't it?"

The man didn't answer, but walked over to the telephone on Doll's desk, picked it up, listened for a second, then slammed it down again, saying something unpleasant under his breath.

"Can you fix it?" Andy said.

"Might be the exchange."

"Might be—but I think that you'd better check it through, anyway."

The man nodded and went to walk out of the room; then he remembered that his door was open and he came back to lock it. He waited until Andy had stepped into the corridor and then he locked Doll's door too and watched Andy walk away.

Not that Andy walked very far. Once in the hall he sat in an easy chair and counted off the seconds on his watch. He came back into the corridor, saw that the coast was clear, and unlocked Doll's door. The other lock was trickier, and he was beginning to sweat with the hurried effort of the job, but it yielded to him at last.

The room was surprisingly large. One side was covered by a massive bank of television screens, most of which showed empty rooms and the dark grounds of the school. Andy grinned as, on one screen, he saw the controller trying to trace the telephone wires from the switchboard. That'll keep you out of mischief for a while yet, friend, he thought. The wall facing him was hidden by curtains: yet, on the ledge in front of the curtains there was a microphone and a panel of switches. He chose one, flicked it, and the curtains slid silently open. He was now looking through a long window on to the squash court. Nodding happily, he switched the curtains back into place.

On the left-hand wall there was a range of metal cupboards. He opened one up and saw that its shelves were filled with row upon row of video cassettes, each bearing the name of one of the pupils. He had to open three of the cupboards before he came to Martin's name. He noticed that he seemed to have more cassettes than anyone else. He took the cassettes out of the boxes and slipped them into his pocket.

The rest of the space was taken up with a computer terminal and a telex machine, by the side of which was a safe. He knew that there'd be no point in trying to force that one: it was a job for someone with a great deal more time and skill than he possessed.

On one of the screens he saw that supper was ending, and so knew he'd better be on his way. He took a random collection of cassette boxes out of the cupboard and changed the contents round from box to box, putting a few into Martin's empty boxes.

Not a bad night's work, he thought, as he got back to his own room, not bad at all! Tomorrow morning would be home movie time and then, maybe, he'd know a bit more about Martin Smith.

# TEN

Borrowing a video player was no problem—at Falconleigh you were thought of as odd if you didn't borrow equipment, rather than if you did.

Andy wedged a chair against the door handle, slipped on a pair of headphones and settled down to watch the tapes. They were all of Martin's "Games" with Farley . . . and, as Andy saw the boy's torment grow, it was hard for him to keep to the cool responses proper for an Intelligence Officer. What they were doing to that kid was damnable, and he fervently hoped that the lot of them would burn in hell for it!.

He tried to remember the lectures he'd had from psychologists when he was being trained—was it possible to put right the damage that had been done to the boy's mind? Possibly, he thought, but only possibly. Of course, he should be in the care of a decent psycho-analyst: but to get him to one meant getting him out of Falconleigh, and, as he'd seen, there was no way of doing that without bringing on such a massive trauma that his mind could be blasted for ever.

Whatever was going to be done for Martin Smith would have to be done here, and by himself. But was he competent to do it? Could he dare take the terrible risks?

He sat for a long time thinking. Then he put the cassettes in his pocket and took his car keys from the shelf. He had some shopping to do.

\*

The afternoon sunlight streamed into Martin's room, but his desk lamp was still lit. Andy leant over his shoulder and switched it off, but the boy scarcely noticed him and went on writing. Gently, Andy took the pencil from his hand. Martin didn't respond, even to this, but stared at the figures on his paper. Andy laid a hand on his shoulder. "You been to bed yet?" he asked.

"When I've finished."

Andy nodded and moved away. "I've got the rock group tape you asked for."

"That's good," Martin said, blankly.

The cassette player was on the floor, by the cushions. Andy pushed the tape in and started it up. He knew how long he'd have from now on, and the sound of the music would shield what he had to say from the ears of the ever-listening controller. He went back to Martin. "How much more work is there in this?"

"I don't know . . ." Still that dead, totally exhausted voice. "It's like going for a long walk . . . you climb a hill . . . then there's another hill . . ."

"Try too many in one day and your legs give out."

Martin didn't reply, but looked down again at his notes. He rubbed his brow, frowning against the light. "This stuff's good though . . ."

"Is it?"

"I think so."

"Then, how near are you?"

"You don't really get all that far, you know. I mean, there's never any sudden breakthrough. Days of it . . . days . . . pushing really hard . . . and it resists, shoving you back. But, at the finish, you've moved—only one step, but you've moved."

"I've never known any of this," Andy said, so quietly

131

that Martin could scarcely hear him over the beat of the rock group.

"Some days—weeks maybe—you've actually moved back. You get fed up then."

"You know where you're going, though?"

Martin shook his head. "Where I'm going? Aye, I suppose I do: but that's like Mount Everest—and there's still all the foothills between me and it."

Andy stood behind him, hands on the back of his chair, mouth close to his ear. "The German word for rubbish is 'quark'. Right?"

"So they say . . ."

"But what you'll finish up with . . . Mount Everest . . . *that* won't be rubbish, will it Martin? The super bomb . . . that's not just final destination for you, is it? It's *all* our endings . . ."

Martin looked out of the window, then shut his eyes: the sunlight was painful to him. "Only out there . . . out there is . . ."

"Is what, Martin, is *what* out there?"

"In the trees, in the streets. Not leaves, but black rags blowing . . ." He turned to Andy, gripping his arms tightly. "Can't you smell it? Taste it? Dying, dying and everything broken, spoiled!"

"And here, at Falconleigh?" Andy said, his voice gentle.

Martin turned back to his table and fussily boxed his papers into a neat pile. "Clean. No one spoiling, taking and trampling. *No one using!*" He turned to Andy again, and he was trembling with his force of feeling. "Have you ever had an idea that's never been in anyone's head before yours? Hasn't been greasy fingered?"

"No. If that's a pleasure, I've never had it."

"Then you haven't lived. Not for a minute."

"I'll take your word for it." The rock group were into

their third number. He hadn't any more time. "Like the tape I got you?" he said.

Martin shrugged. "It's all right. It's a shutting out noise . . . that's all I want."

"Leave you to it, then." And he went.

In the corridor, he took a look at his watch—he had less than two minutes. Luckily for him, the corridor was deserted. He ran his hands along the wall over the door and, taking a small knife from his pocket, prised open an electrician's panel. He could see the camera lead branching into the room. Working fast he stripped the plastic off the wire, trying to make it look as if it had frayed naturally. He slipped the panel back: at least now, Falconleigh would be blind and deaf.

He leant against the closed door and waited, counting the seconds off with a beat of his index finger on an open palm. The rock group was still playing. Then the music stopped: there would be a one point five second pause . . . now! And the air was filled with the screams of a great bird in its death agony, raucous, terrifying, like hooked talons ripping into your mind. For three more seconds of that hellish shrieking he held tight on to the door handle, slippery now with the sweat of his hands; then he threw the door open, mortally afraid of what he might see. And it was terrible enough, God knows. Martin was on the floor and cowering, in a corner of the room, his hands covering his ears, and his screams one with the bird's. His face was masked by such total terror that, for a moment, Andy couldn't move to help him. Then he ran to the cassette player, switched its nightmare off and threw it to the ground with such force that the casing smashed. He ran over to Martin, trying to pick him up, but he was clumsy and only managed to get him upright.

"Martin! Martin!" he shouted. "That's Falconleigh!

That's what this place is! That's what it's doing to you! You know it! Don't you?"

Martin didn't answer him, sobbing and twisting, fighting to get away.

"The killers aren't just in the world outside these trees. They're here too ... and you'll never escape them by staying in this room in this place. They're death men and they're holding fast to you! Leave them, Martin and go to the men of life! Life or death—everyone turns to one or the other and becomes what he has chosen. Where do you belong, Martin? *Where do you belong?* You can't shut yourself away, for then you've made no choice—but the death men will take your stillness and silence for 'yes', because you haven't said 'no'."

Martin was quiet now, but his eyes were still shut and he was rocking backwards and forwards where he sat.

Andy got to his feet and looked down at him. "Noise that you heard—it was a nail scraped against a piece of tin. I'm no death man."

Martin didn't answer or look at him.

"You asked me if I'd ever had a completely original thought. I don't suppose I have. And I call myself a scientist, so that's the pity of me, isn't it? But *you* have—my God, you have—and those thoughts of yours are free, flying high. But the death men want them, and they're taking them, binding them, locking them into a steel case. And that case will become a most obscene bomb. They will make it so. And this is happening now. Here. At Falconleigh."

"No!" Martin's shout was torn from the very centre of his being.

"Yes, Martin! *Yes!*" Andy was at his side again, desperate in his fear that he was losing some gigantic epic battle that had to be won. "That hurt has to be taken! You saw a bird killed by flying near a laser beam, and it was here at Falconleigh! *You saw that. Didn't you?*"

"No! No! They told me—they—"

"Injections!" He grabbed the boy's thin arm and tore the shirt sleeve back—there were the needle marks. "Look!" But Martin turned his face away. "Drugs and deep hypnosis! They're making you their zombie! Don't you realise that? You're programmed on a path of self-destruction because they want their bomb in a hurry. So you work for them without food and without sleep until you climb your Mount Everest: but when you've done that, and you're at your last breath and you look down from that high peak, what sort of world will you see, Martin? A world of grey dust and poisoned air? *Made by you?*"

Martin's body suddenly relaxed: it was as if a spring had been snapped. He got up and walked to his table, picked up his notes and held them towards Andy. "Supposing I told you," he said, his voice firm and calm, "that these papers filled in the last theoretical gap between you and the making of this bomb. What would you do with them?"

Andy knew that everything was at stake now, and hung upon his answer; but his mind was tired and he couldn't think what that answer should be. He played for time. "I can't destroy your thought. That's not possible."

Martin saw the evasion and smiled. "So long as you let me go on living! No, it's not. But that's not the answer. *Is it?*"

"I'd see that your thoughts weren't heard by the wrong people."

"Wrong people. Right people. And you to decide?"

Andy gave an almost imperceptible nod.

"Of course. And the bomb would get made. Wouldn't it? By the right people. And then they'd kill all the wrong people. You're a lousy stink in my nose, Mr Rutherford."

Andy was beaten. The battle was finished and the corpses were everywhere. "The main thing at this minute . . ."

*"It would be made and used! Wouldn't it?"*

" . . . is to get you out of here . . !"

"No! The main thing is to get *you* out of here! Go on! Get out!"

"Martin, I want to help you!"

"There's no help from anyone!" He held his notes close in his arms. "All I've got, all I am, is on this paper! There's nothing else!" He sat down at his table, straightened the papers and started to work.

"Listen!"

"You've nothing to say that I want to hear." The pencil was in his hand and writing. Andy stood behind him, helpless. For the sake of the world he knew what he had to do now. Slowly his hand went up to his shoulder holster —and now the weight of the gun was cold and heavy in it. He slipped the safety catch off and lifted his arm.

Perhaps Martin heard the sound of the catch moving: certainly, his head came up, and there was something in that movement that stopped Andy. He couldn't do it —whatever the cost, the action was beyond him. He put the gun back and Martin turned to face him; and there was such a look of contempt in his eyes that Andy dropped his gaze and walked out of the room.

*

It was growing dark, but Andy didn't notice as he sat on the edge of his bed and considered the ruin of his plans. There was no way forward. The Icarus Foundation had defeated him: he should have known that it would, for it was impregnable.

He began to pack his case. No point in hanging on now: there was nothing more that could happen. As soon as it was completely dark he would go. It wasn't the first time in his life that he'd been beaten, but it was the bitterest.

*

Martin put his pencil down and sat back. The circle of light from his lamp surrounded him. "So far . . . so *far*," he whispered.

He carefully picked up the papers, got up from the chair, and carried them to the centre of the room, like a priest performing some solemn rite. He knelt, putting the papers by the side of a tea tray on the floor. He took a box of matches from his pocket, struck one and held it until the flame was sure. Then he took the top sheet of paper and held the match under it, watching the figures blacken and twist in the flame. He let the burning scrap fall on to the tray. He took the next sheet and lit it from the flame of the first . . . and the third sheet followed them.

So intent was he on his task, that he didn't notice the door open or see the person standing in the darkness.

Then Sue spoke. "Had you finished it, then?"

He didn't look up. "No. Further than anyone's got. I don't know how much more there'd be."

She knelt beside him and stirred the ashes with her finger. "That's what I've been doing too . . ."

*

It was time. Andy slid his room window up and dropped his case on to the flower bed below: pity he couldn't jump after it, he thought: but the height was too great. He walked to the door, opened it a fraction and looked out. The corridor was empty and he closed the door behind him and walked towards the hall.

He had almost got to the main entrance, when a voice behind him said "Going somewhere, Mr Rutherford?"

He turned, keeping himself relaxed: "Thought I'd take a breath of air."

"What a good idea," Doll said, "but I wonder if you could spare me a moment or two first?"

Andy shrugged and followed him into his office. As he did so, the door slammed shut behind him and the controller leant against it . . . and Andy didn't like the look in his eyes, or the way in which his right hand was thrust deep into his jacket pocket.

Doll didn't speak until he was seated behind his desk. He waved Andy into the facing chair. "Now," he said, very comfortably, "I wonder if you'd mind telling me who you're working for?"

"Obvious," Andy smiled.

Doll shook his head, regretfully. "No. I'm afraid it's not." He looked thoughtfully at Andy before he spoke again. "You see, your cover's blown, Commander."

"Ah," Andy sighed, still smiling.

Doll opened the top drawer of his desk, as if he were looking for some trivial piece of paper; but it was a revolver that he took out and placed on his leather blotting pad, his finger lightly over the trigger. "I suppose that you too have a gun—would you be kind enough to place it by the side of this one please?"

Andy turned to look at the controller. As he had sensed, the man was holding a Smith and Wesson. Both hands firm; arms straight, the barrel pointing at the base of Andy's skull. This lad knows what he's at, he thought, as he slipped his own gun from its holster and on to the desk.

"I was in the village this afternoon," Doll went on, "and I took the opportunity of making a couple of phone calls. Your friend Madge can't interfere with every telephone in the kingdom, alas, so I was able to get through to our real headquarters. They made some enquiries on our behalf . . . and here we are."

"Indeed we are."

"Now—where's Peter Farley?"

"Safe."

"Unlike you."

"Quite."

"As a matter of interest . . . we had you taken off your investigation. Suspended. So what brought you meddling?"

"Guesswork."

"Clever—or it would be if you were capable of it. I repeat my question: who are you working for?"

"You've got the best brains in the country here—surely you could find that out for yourselves?"

"Surely . . . but what I'd propose to you is this: that you leave their service, have a lapse of memory and go back to your office—returning Peter Farley to us on the way. I think that you'll find that your superiors are quite prepared to forgive and forget."

"That's a very nice thought, but you see, the trouble is that I'm cursed with a very good memory. And I remember British missiles being blown out of the air by your lasers. I don't like that." Out of the corner of his eye he could see the controller moving nearer to him. "And I don't care if the whole of the Security Service is in your pocket—I'm still going to stop you."

"You're not, you know," Doll murmured.

Andy saw his chance—not much of one, it was true, but all that was on offer. The controller had placed himself just behind his chair, and Andy threw himself down and round, so that his shoulder hit the man's stomach. He doubled up, gasping with the shock of the blow, and Andy took the weight of him, turned and heaved him over the desk. The guns and the lamp went flying and the room was dark. Keeping low, he threw himself towards the door. Thank God, the man hadn't locked it, and Andy grabbed the key, got out, slammed the door behind him, held it shut against a pull from inside while he got the key into the lock and turned it. But he'd scarcely done it when he heard the revolver shot. Instinctively, he threw himself to the ground and then looked up to see the bullet hole in the woodwork. He scrambled to his feet and ran for the hall, getting his car keys out as he went. The night air was sweet and he gulped a breath of it as he ran towards the car park.

He got to his car. To his relief it wasn't boxed in—let's just hope and pray that it starts first time, he thought. In his haste he dropped the keys, and, as he was scrabbling in the gravel for them he heard another shot from the house. That'll be the lock, he thought, as he found his keys. He threw himself into the driving seat, pulled the choke out and turned the key. The engine coughed a couple of times, but then it fired. He banged the gear lever into reverse and roared back. He was clear now: into first and he was away, spouts of stones thrown out behind him. He'd just got the car into top and the needle was flicking on the sixty mark, when his lights picked up the white faces of two people in front of him. He was about to accelerate more when he recognised one of those faces. With all his strength he rammed the brake pedal down, but the tyres hadn't enough grip on the gravel and he went into a screaming skid, turning completely round, then going back end first off the drive and on to the grass. Whether he'd hit them or not he couldn't tell—he'd lost sight of them and his headlights were pointing in the wrong direction. Winding the window down as he swung on the wheel, he got the car back on to the drive. From the house he heard another shot. Not at this range, chummy, he thought. Then his headlights picked up the figures he'd seen, and they were still running. He'd been right: it *was* Sue and Martin.

He drove after them, shouting through the open window:

"Martin! Martin! Stay where you are!" He was nearly on them now, but the kids weren't stopping. "In the car, man! I'll get you out!" He leant across to open the passenger door, swerving wildly as he did it, but still they ignored him. He braked and jumped out.

Martin turned to him. "Not with you!" he shouted. "On my own!"

Andy looked over his shoulder at the school. He could hear a car starting up—they were running out of time and luck. Then he looked back at Martin—the kid was all in, stumbling and weaving. "All right!" Andy bellowed. "But run! Run!"

And Martin was almost on the edge of the estate now: another few yards and he'd be out. Then, to Andy's horror, he stopped, swaying as if he was about to collapse. Andy ran up to him, putting an arm round his shoulders to help him, but the boy shoved him away, and Andy knew, by the look of abject terror on his face, that the fear of the world that had been twisted into his mind had him firmly in its grip. There was nothing that would get him across that invisible line: you might as well ask a man to jump into a foaming whirlpool. Sue was pulling at his arm and shouting: "Please, Martin! Please! It's all right, it's all right." But there was no moving him. There was nothing for Andy to do but to get back to his car and save himself—the boy was lost.

Then there was a great shout from the trees: it was a voice that Andy had almost forgotten, but Martin hadn't. He stopped struggling against Sue and stood, staring at the boundary, unable to believe what he was hearing.

"Martin!" the voice was shouting, and it was getting nearer, there was the sound of someone crashing through the undergrowth. "Come on, our kid! We're going home!"

"Barry! Barry!" Martin sobbed. "Where are you?" He

was running now, towards the trees, Sue after him. Then he was through, breaking the barrier that had held him prisoner.

Andy leapt into his car and drove fast through the gates. He was alongside the kids now and squealed to a stop. "Get in!" he cried. "And be quick about it!" The other car was coming fast down the drive now: another few seconds and it would be on them. All three fell into the back of the car, thrown down by the force of the acceleration.

Andy's hobby was rally driving and he was good at it. He took those narrow, twisting country lanes as if the hedges had been greased. The controller had no chance—his nerve gave out after the first mile and when they came to a crossroads with neither sight nor sound of Andy's car, he slowed to a halt.

"Get back to the school," Doll shouted. "There's a lot of things we've got to be doing . . ."

# ELEVEN

Naval Intelligence has at its disposal five "Safe Houses" in various parts of the country. They are useful properties, unknown to anyone outside the Service and always available when someone from the other side has to be questioned, when secret meetings have to be held or when an angry and frightened Physics master from a dodgy special school has to be kept out of play for a week or two.

It was in one of these houses that Ted and Harold passed the time as best they could while keeping an eye on Peter Farley. It was boring work, but they had done a fair bit of it in their time and took it in their stride. And the house wasn't unpleasant. There were splendid views of the sea from the main bedroom and, which was rather more important, a completely uninterrupted view of the approach road from the living-room. Harold was in this living-room when he first glimpsed the headlights of Andy's car. He nodded towards Ted and they took up their positions—Harold behind the door, pressed flat against the wall, gun held easy in his hand, and Ted at the table, apparently engrossed by a paperback thriller. When the door burst open and Andy and the kids came in, Harold slammed the door behind them, but Ted merely looked up and said: "Fancy something to eat? I could open a tin of something." Coolness was their invariable style. But their eyes missed nothing as Sue led Martin to a chair and gently sat him down. Ted flicked a glance towards Andy as he saw the state of the boy . . . for it was obvious that he was in a bad way, white as a sheet and trembling. Andy shook his head and Barry looked down at his brother, his face clouded with rage.

"How've they got him like this?" he said.

"Drugs. Hypnosis," Andy replied.

"Will he get better?"

"With treatment . . . I think so."

Barry's voice was low, but very dangerous. "I'd like five minutes on my own with them that did it . . ."

"Wouldn't we all! Meantime, get him to bed. And keep an eye on him, whatever you do, keep an eye on him."

"We'll watch him," Harold said.

Andy was already making for the door. "Where you off to now, then?" Ted asked.

"Business, in London. Back tomorrow," was all the reply they got.

*

The dining-room at Falconleigh was crowded: all the pupils and staff were there, some in pyjamas and dressing-gowns, some in such clothes as they had hurriedly put on. They were sitting on tables and standing round the room in small groups. Doll was about to speak to them when the controller came to his side.

"I managed to contact the boss," he said.

"And?"

"He's on his way. He says do nothing until he arrives."

"It isn't the time for doing nothing." He turned to the people in the room. "Sorry to drag you from your beds, but I needed to talk to you. I'm sure that you all heard some shooting earlier on. Dreadful business. It seems that there's some sort of terrorist group with a grudge against us here at Falconleigh—as a matter of fact one of them took a couple of shots at me. So, quite clearly they're not kidding." There

144

was an outbreak of noise at this, but Doll put up his hand to silence it. "The police are doing their best to round these nutters up . . . but in the meantime, for the safety of all of us, they advise a 'strategic withdrawal'. In plain language that means a holiday for everyone at the Icarus school in France! There'll be coaches here in two hours' time, our flight leaves Heathrow in the morning and it's all the delights of French cooking by lunch . . ."

\*

When Andy arrived, Sir Hugh's dinner guests had just gone, and he sat in the dining-room among the remains of the food. "Pour yourself a glass of port, Andy," was his only greeting.

Andy sat opposite him and filled a glass.

"How were things at Falconleigh, then?"

"Was it John Doll who tipped you off?"

"No. It wasn't. And you must reflect on the fact that I'd be a very poor Head of Intelligence if I didn't know where my own people were."

"Someone told them . . ."

"Indeed they did. We have some very rotten apples in the barrel, but I am not one of them. So: make your report."

Andy did: in the teeth of the evidence, he trusted this man—that was a habit that couldn't be broken. At last he finished, and Sir Hugh walked over to the window, pulling the curtains back. The light of early morning filled the room, making the guttering candles seem tawdry. "Promises a fine day," he said.

"After a long night."

"Yes . . ."

"So . . . what do you think?"

Sir Hugh turned to face him. "I think that you have made a monumental nonsense of the whole thing."

"Now just a minute!" Andy cried.

"First of all you disobeyed my most explicit order—but we'll leave that aside for the moment. Infinitely more damaging is the fact that, by your clumsy blundering, you have wrecked long and delicate investigations into the world-wide operations of the Icarus Foundation . . . you have, as it were, blown on the web, and the spider will have scuttled away—"

"The spider?"

"My dear chap—someone set up this Foundation and, for aught I know, controls it now. But who? Thanks to you, we're going to be a long time finding out."

"I'm sorry."

"So you should be. Point is, can we save anything from the ruin?"

"We could arrest the lot."

"On what charge? Scientific enquiry? I wasn't aware that that was a criminal offence."

"What they did to young Smith . . ."

"Damnable, I quite agree, but you can bet your bottom dollar that those drugs were administered by a qualified doctor, and he'd swear that they were part of the treatment." Sir Hugh took a nut from a silver bowl and cracked it. "Of course, we *do* have the boy—and, presumably, they want him back . . ."

"Use him as bait?"

"Possibly . . . that might bring the big spider running. I'll put the word out to a few of my dodgier colleagues. And we'll see what happens. After that we'll take a drive in the country. Attractive part of the world, is it . . . ? Where this safe house of ours is . . . ?"

*

Sue and Barry were having their second cup of coffee after breakfast. Martin was sitting by the fire, bent over his papers and writing.

"Doesn't he ever give up?" Barry said.

"I thought he'd left the work, but it looks as if he's back on it again," she replied.

Ted clattered downstairs, carrying a tray of plates. "Prisoner eat a hearty breakfast?" Harold asked him.

"Still grumbling. Some folk are never satisfied."

Barry got up from the table, stretched himself and looked at Sue. "Fancy a walk," he said. "Bit of exercise?"

She nodded.

"Not too far," Harold warned.

"It's all right," Ted said. "I'll keep an eye on them." He turned to Barry. "You two walk along the beach . . . I'll take a stroll on the cliffs. That way we'll all be OK."

*

Doll's visitor was with him again, and they were both in the control room at Falconleigh. The man was talking to someone on the phone, and, by his expression, the news that he was getting was to his satisfaction. He put the phone down and smiled at Doll. "Icarus has good friends," he said.

"The boy—have they told you where he is?"

"Of course. And now I need a map."

Doll walked over to a drawer on the other side of the room. "Big scale map of this area. That do for you?"

The man took the map and spread it out. "This safe house of theirs . . . it's about four-and-a-half miles away. See . . ."

Doll leant over his shoulder. "So what do we do? Go out and get him?"

The man laughed. "You are a fool, Mr Doll! It is à trap! Can't you see that?"

"You said that our informant was reliable!"

"So he is—but you must ask yourself who told *him* that the boy was there?"

"All right!" Doll said, sitting down. "But what are we to do? We can't just sit here, waiting for something to happen . . ."

"Why not?"

"Because what *will* happen is that someone will come up that drive and arrest us."

"On what charge?"

"If it's a question of shutting this place up, they'll soon invent one."

The man sat back in his chair, head on one side, looking at Doll like a hesitant customer in a shop, wondering whether to buy. "Do you wish to leave, Mr Doll?"

"I want that boy back—once we've got him . . ."

"Why? Why do you want him?"

"Obvious, because of what he knows, what he holds in his mind. The power that he will give us . . ."

"These are not good reasons for keeping a human being near you."

"Have you any better?"

"I hope so."

There was silence between them: the man looking steadily at Doll the while and tapping his pencil on the map. Then he spoke. "You should go, Mr Doll. I have no doubt of that in my mind. Leave here, and that quickly!"

"What's brought this about?"

The man shook his head. "There is nothing here for you any more . . ."

"Now, listen . . ."

"An order. You will go . . ."

Doll knew that there was no arguing against the finality in that man's voice. "I could join the rest of the Falconleigh children at the Paris school . . ."

The grey-haired man frowned briefly at Doll, then looked away and shook his head. "No."

"Where then? Where shall I go . . . ?"

"The pilot of my helicopter has been told to be ready for take off in five minutes. He will take you wherever you wish . . . but not to an Icarus school. That part of your life is over."

"And you?"

"I have an appointment. I must be here to keep it."

*

The late sunshine had a touch of warmth in it and Harold was sitting in the open doorway. Martin's notes were spread over the table, and he was leaning back in his chair, a hand on each edge of the table, looking at them.

"That it should be so obvious," he murmured. "In my hand all the time . . ."

"You say something?" Harold called.

'No. Nothing." And he straightened the papers.

Harold heard the scrape of Martin's chair as he pushed it back.

"Where you off to now?" he said.

"Upstairs—the loo."

"OK."

No need to worry. Farley was safe enough—feet tied, wrists handcuffed to the bed post. Harold went back to his sun-bathing.

The door to Farley's room was open: he saw Martin go past, then, after a couple of minutes, he heard the sound of the lavatory flushing. He heard Martin come back along the passage.

"Martin!"

Martin stopped in the doorway and looked in at him.

"What?"

"There's a glass in the bathroom . . . could you fetch me some water, please?"

Martin hesitated—he didn't want anything to do with

this—it was the job of the guy downstairs. "I'll fetch Harold."

Farley smiled. "Don't be daft, Martin! What possible harm could there be in giving a glass of water to a middle-aged, out-of-conditon schoolmaster who's tied hand and foot?"

Martin didn't smile back, but he went to fetch the water. He came back into the room, carrying the brimming glass.

"You'll have to feed it to me, I'm afraid." Martin leant over the bed and held the glass to his lips. Farley nodded after he'd taken a couple of mouthfuls and Martin took the glass away. "Thanks. I'll just take a breather, then I'll have another sip, if I may."

Martin looked down at him, dispassionately.

"How's the work going, then?" Farley said.

"All right."

\*

Ted had kept a careful eye on Barry and Sue, and as they turned for home, he was glad to follow them back; it was blooming cold once you were out of shelter.

Sue got back to the house first. She saw Harold sitting in the sun and called out to him as she came up the path: "How's Martin?"

"Fine! Seems to have finished his writing anyway. I heard him in the kitchen a minute since, making a cuppa, probably . . ."

She walked through to the kitchen and the first thing she saw was the window: it was open and swinging on its hinges in the wind. She was gripped by a spasm of fear that was like a pain in her chest. She ran back into the living-room. Barry and Ted had just walked in and they were laughing at some joke that Harold had made.

"He's not there!" she cried.

They turned slowly towards her, their faces blank, unbelieving.

"Upstairs, then," Harold said, and she saw that he had
caught her fear.

Ted pushed past him and went up the stairs two at a
time, and they waited in silence, hoping against hope that
they would hear Martin's voice speaking to him. But when
Ted came downstairs again he was on his own.

"He's gone," he said. "The kid's gone!"

No one spoke or moved.

"So what the hell do we do now?" Ted asked.

*

Martin plunged through the bracken and the clutching
briars: his clothes were torn and his face and arms lined
with scratches. He was sucking air into his lungs like a
long-distance runner at the end of a race. Surely, it couldn't
be far now—soon, soon he would see the golden light on the
grass and the sheltering trees. Soon . . .

*

After Andy's explosion of rage against Harold, the room
had gone quiet again. Ted and Harold had done all that
could be done before Andy got there: the police were out in
force, there were road blocks circling the area, every bus
and railway station was being watched, even the coast-
guards had been alerted.

Sir Hugh sipped his coffee and looked round. "They'll
pick him up," he said. "Merely a question of time."

Sue was standing at the window, looking out. "No. They
won't. Because he's cleverer than any of you. Don't you
know that yet?"

"At his own thing—I dare say he is," Andy said.

Sue turned to look at him. These people weren't fit to
breathe Martin's air, she thought. And that reminded her
of the bird—and that reminded her—she gripped the back

of a chair so tightly that her knuckles went white; her head went down and she swayed forward. Andy thought that she was going to faint and moved to catch her, but she shook him off and sat down. "I know where he is . . ." she whispered.

*

Martin stood in the Games Room, swaying on his feet. He could scarcely see; the walls of the room came near, then went away again. He was trying to understand the emptiness of the school—he needed these people and they had deserted him. He thought that if he shouted loudly enough, someone would hear him and come to help.

He lifted his head up. 'Mr Doll! Jacko! Please, Jacko!" But there was only the echo of his cry. "Don't let me be on my own, Jacko! Please!"

There could be no answer, and he was beginning to know it, but he made a last effort and cried again: "I've come back! That's what you wanted! Don't send me away again, don't . . ."

Out of the darkness at the end of the room he heard a man's voice—heavy and accented.

It was saying his name, over and over. "Martin . . . Martin . . ."

This wasn't part of Falconleigh, this was someone else, someone who would use him. He turned and ran towards the door, but the door was going further and further away.

"Stay where you are! This is the only safe place for you!"

And Martin stopped. "I don't know who you are! I want Mr Doll . . . the others . . ."

Hands were gripping his shoulders now, stopping him from falling. "They will be back," the man was saying. "I am left to look after you—to save you from what is out there. Come, sit. Bring your head down, between your knees. That is good. You will soon feel better."

His eyes began to clear; he saw his mud-stained shoes and torn trousers. He lifted his head and saw that the man was offering him a glass of some golden liquid.

"Brandy. You see, I was ready for you. Drink it, it will help." Martin took a gulp from the glass, but it burned his throat and made him choke. "Now the water," the man was saying, giving him another glass. This time Martin drank greedily, gulping the water down.

The man smiled at him—Martin had a memory of seeing his face somewhere . . . somewhere important to him. "Who are you?" he whispered.

"In a moment. But first we must talk about you, for I know you so well, Martin. Like a father, I have followed every turn, every twist of your work. It was I who set its direction; but this was not hard for me, for we are of the same blood, you and I, we have trodden the same path . . ."

Martin shook his head . . . if only he could remember . . .

"In school, I too knew the bitter unhappy years—until they threw me out of that terrible place. They said that I was a 'disruptive influence'. But my path went on, as yours will, and, ten years later, I had been given the Nobel Prize. Until you, I was the youngest ever . . . for you are going to beat me in that."

It came back to Martin then; a photograph in a physics book, dog-eared with handling, of a young man standing in front of a cheering audience and holding a golden medal carelessly in his hands.

But it couldn't be! It couldn't be!

"Froelich. Edward Froelich," he whispered. Then he shut his eyes against the ghost. "And this is another Falconleigh Game . . . and I can't play any more. Please, if you have any pity, whoever you are, fetch John Doll to me."

"No game," the man said, putting his hands across the table and on to Martin's. "I am Edward Froelich."

Martin still didn't look at him. "A lie! He was killed in the war. We killed him. I know that."

"And I tell you that I am no ghost. I speak truth to you, for that is what a scientist does—and there is no time for anything else."

Martin looked up at him. "If you are that man, I have to tell you that you were my idol; through all those grey years."

Froelich nodded, accepting this. "The same blood . . . we have a great gift, you and I—and to how few is that gift given. In all of time we are a small light in a great darkness. And this gift must not be lost, not be wasted. That is the great truth for us, isn't it, Martin?"

"How did you know?" Martin whispered.

"Because I wasted my gift. I put out that light."

"Why?"

"In the face of a great evil I thought that I had no choice. The Nazis were in power in my country. They wanted an atomic bomb . . . and they knew that I could give it to them."

"But you didn't."

"The scientist is the truth teller. Always. But I told lie upon lie, twisted my research, corrupted my experiments, until they gave up their search for the bomb. And that is how you come to be alive now, Martin. Then my lab was bombed by your Air Force. It was thought that I was dead, buried under the ruins, and I let them think that, for now I was free, free of lying, free to go back to the sweet truth of my work . . . but . . ."

"The gift was gone . . . wasted . . . ?"

Froelich nodded.

"But that wasn't your only choice," Martin said. "You could have told the truth and said 'no'."

"Would *you* have done?"

Martin thought for a long time before he spoke. "I don't know. I'd have wanted to."

"But . . . for me . . ." He shrugged his shoulders. "And now, here I was, second only to Einstein in this century and unable to see further than some plodding student. I had nothing left . . . except my hate for those men of power, wherever they were, who had so used science. And so I decided that I would use *them*. With my Icarus Foundation I would keep my children free, untainted, and their work I would sell to the highest bidder. But the money from this would always go back to the children, to give them whatever they wanted. And I sold, to this side and that, keeping those men in a dance of fear."

Martin shook his head wearily. "You should never have done that. It was wrong."

"You judge?"

"No. I don't. Not judge. *But you used us*. Made us part of your hate. And we didn't know."

In the far distance, a police siren sounded, but neither of them heard it.

"Icarus. Icarus," Martin murmured. "So beautiful."

There was silence before Martin spoke again: "But there must be no more of Icarus. It must finish."

"It is finished now! You are the sum of it! With this bomb of yours we will have all the power of history in our hands! And I will give you everything . . . work space, equipment, assistants . . ."

When Martin spoke, his words came slowly, as if each one cost him a great effort. "You are dead. I know you are. The books tell me so, and I believe them. And you must keep away from my living. I am not a stick for a corpse to beat the world with."

"No! No, Martin!" Froelich cried. "To make the world beautiful! Perfect!"

"Like Falconleigh?" Martin shouted back.

The police siren was nearer now. They both heard it, but they didn't take their eyes off each other.

"Without me your work will never be complete."

In reply, Martin took a bundle of papers from his pocket and threw them on to the table. "You're too late. It's all there."

"Finished?" Froelich whispered.

"Finished."

Froelich went to pick the papers up, but his fingers drew back from touching them.

"And now . . . what will you do with it, Martin . . . ?"

"I don't know."

Froelich placed a box of matches next to the papers. "You could burn . . . destroy."

Martin took up the matches and opened the box. "Yes," he said. "I could. Or I could put them back in my pocket. But it's going to be my choice—not yours."

Froelich looked towards the doors, and knew that his time was gone. "I have to go now," he said. "But I give you one more chance."

Martin was on his feet, holding on to the table. He shook his head.

Froelich took something from his pocket and laid it on the table. "You turn from the large offer—accept, then, a small gift."

Martin looked at the newspaper-wrapped bundle. "What is it?" he asked.

"The Nobel Peace Prize Medal."

He pulled the paper away and looked at the golden glory of it, then touched it, feeling the raised surface under his finger tips. "Thank you," he said.

They could hear footsteps, running, along the path outside the building.

"I'm cured now of Falconleigh," Martin said.

"It was never meant to be an illness: my Icarus was always safe."

"But I am not Icarus. We're different." He took the papers and the medal and put them in his pocket. "I don't fear the sun. I hold it."

The doors at the back of the room were thrown open and a shaft of light held them. Froelich turned his head away —it was blinding him.

"Martin!" Andy shouted. "Who is that man?"

Martin looked at Andy, then at Froelich. Without speaking, he walked out of the Games Room and into the corridor.

Outside the door there was a wastepaper basket. He took something from his pocket and thrust it deep into the rubbish.

Through a window he could see Barry and Sue waiting in the drive: he started to run towards them.

This story is based on the BBC TV series Codename Icarus first shown in 1981. It was produced by Paul Stone and directed by Marilyn Fox. The main characters who appear in the book were played as follows: Martin Smith, Barry Angel; Barry Smith, Steven Mann; Sue Kleiner, Debbie Farrington; John Doll, Philip Locke; Andy Rutherford, Jack Galloway; Edward Froelich, John Malcolm.